Burning Desire and Other Stories

Marilyn Todd

Published by Untreed Reads, 2023.

"Awaiting the Dawn": *Mammoth Book of Dickensian Mysteries*, 2007

"Burning Desire": *Ellery Queen's Mystery Magazine*, Sept/Oct 2020, reprinted in "Best Mysteries of 2021" edited by Lee Child

"Night Crossing": *Ellery Queen's Mystery Magazine*, July/Aug 2017

"Pirate of Penance": *The Beat of Black Wings*, Untreed Reads, Mar 2020

"China Mary": *Ellery Queen's Mystery Magazine*, May/June 2017

"School of Hard Rocks": *Ellery Queen's Mystery Magazine*, Sept/Oct 2019

"The Day of the Jackal": *Ellery Queen's Mystery Magazine*, July/Aug 2019

"The Girl Who Walked on Rooftops": *Ellery Queen's Mystery Magazine*, May 2016

"The Old Man and The Seashore": *Ellery Queen's Mystery Magazine*, Jan 2016, narrated for EQMM's podcast

"Bull's Eye": *Crippen & Landru*, Dec 2017

"Fool's Gold": *Ellery Queen's Mystery Magazine*, Sept/Oct 2017

"Long Slow Dance Through the Passage of Time": *Ellery Queen's Mystery Magazine*, Nov/Dec 2016, narrated for EQMM's November 2021 podcast

"Killing Kevin": *Ellery Queen's Mystery Magazine*, Jan/Feb 2018

"Saw Point": *Ellery Queen's Mystery Magazine*, Mar/April 2016

"A Night in Casablanca": *Monkey Business*, Untreed Reads, Sept 2021

Also by Marilyn Todd and Untreed Reads Publishing
The Claudia Seferius Mysteries
I, Claudia
Virgin Territory
Man Eater
Wolf Whistle
Jail Bait
Black Salamander
Dream Boat
Dark Horse
Second Act
Widow's Pique
Stone Cold
Sour Grapes
Scorpion Rising
The High Priestess Iliona Ancient Greek Mysteries
Blind Eye
Blood Moon
Still Waters
The Wickedest Town in the West and Other Stories
Dead and Breakfast & Other Stories
www.untreedreads.com

Every attempt has been made to present the story as it originally appeared, with British English or American English punctuation and spelling.

AWAITING THE DAWN

S he sat with her back straight, hands clasped in her lap. Had it not been for the cold, or perhaps something else, you would have called her handsome, with her dark hair tied back in a bun and her black satin dress, pinched in at the waist.

Midnight came. One o'clock. Two.

As the cold intensified, the young woman seemed to draw strength from its cruelty, and through the tiny aperture that passed for a window, a solitary star shone in the blackness. Brighter than a turnkey's stare. Elizabeth watched until it moved out of sight, then shifted position ever so slightly. An economy of movement that attracted attention almost as much as the murder itself.

> CENTRAL CRIMINAL COURT, Oct. 2.
> Throughout the proceedings, the prisoner sat, as
> was her custom, as motionless as a statue, looking
> neither to the left nor the right, and was never once
> seen to turn her eyes towards her husband.
>
> *The Times. Oct. 3, 1868.*

Elizabeth fixed on the point where the dawn would eventually brighten. At eight, the prison bell would toll. The chaplain, the governor, the attending surgeon and no less than two turnkeys would accompany the miserable procession towards what yesterday's editorial referred to as *"the awful change."* Her knuckles whitened. Is that what they thought? That placing a cap over someone's head, tightening a rope round their neck, then having the floor drop away equated to nothing more than a shift in personal circumstances?

Her gaze fell to the book lying open beside her. For these past twenty-four days — three clear Sundays being the stipulated interval between sentence being delivered and execution carried out — Elizabeth had had little to do except wait and read, read and wait, wait and read. In the end, she discovered, it was surprisingly easy to overpower reality with a good story, and in this case the book's author was Charles Dickens, its title *Great Expectations*.

The irony of neither was lost.

Subsequent to the hanging he witnessed of another couple who hit the headlines for cold-blooded murder, Mr. Dickens launched a campaign for the abolition of capital punishment. And whilst he was not entirely successful in his endeavours, he was not entirely unsuccessful, either. After nineteen years, Parliament finally compromised by decreeing it should at least be a solemn and intimate affair, business to be carried out within the prison, and away from public jeering and scrutiny. And since this law had only just come into being, newspapermen were apparently obliged to find new ways to fire their readers' interest. Without doubt, a phrase as emotive as *the awful change* would generate debate. Debate, of course, would keep the paper's profile high. More and more copies would be sold.

And there was no denying that William Lacey's violent and untimely end was proving exceedingly profitable for the broadsheets. Love, lust, money, betrayal, this crime contained every ingredient necessary to keep the presses rolling, especially since so many questions remained unanswered.

THE LEXINGTON-PLACE MURDER
EXAMINATION OF MR. AND MRS.
MARKHAM.
The proceedings of the case of Mr. John Albert
Markham, remanded on Tuesday 14th, and of
Elizabeth Markham, his wife, remanded Friday,
17th, resumed yesterday at the Southwark Police
court.
Inspector Haywood stated, in reply to a
question from the bench, that the prisoners had
been permitted an interview. Markham was on
record as stating, "I have nothing to say to my wife."
Mrs. Markham said, "I do not wish to say anything
to him, not one word." The interview lasted under two
minutes.
At 11 o'clock the prisoners, who have both denied
the charge laid against them, were then placed at the
bar. Markham, who was first introduced, was

elevated on a chair on the right-hand side. In contrast, Mrs. Markham was careful to position her chair as far away from her husband as was humanly possible, and did not pass him a look or a token of recognition throughout the day.

The Times. Aug 20th, 1868.

All the world loves a mystery, it makes the front page.

All the world, that is, except for Inspector Haywood, who preferred his solved.

'Until your marriage in June of this year, Mrs. Markham, you were employed in the household of Sir Henry James Wilton, who —' he consulted his notes '— who is in coal, I see.'

Who sucks money from the north so he can wallow in luxury in the south, she thought, and where more food is thrown out in a week than any one of his miners earns in a month.

'That is correct.'

Inspector Haywood. The name conjured up images of a policeman of stature, lean perhaps to the point of bony even, with unruly dark hair and gimlet eyes. In practice, his fringe was thinning, his waistline thickening, he was shorter than Elizabeth and reeked of carbolic soap. Only the gimlet eyes matched her expectations.

'Where you served as a governess to Sir Henry's daughter?'

'Prudence.' A less suitable name for an overindulged, under exercised brat Elizabeth could not imagine. Even at twelve, she was so fat that it was impossible to tell where face finished and shoulders commenced, and what paradox. Calling her after the virtue of restraint in an environment where moderation was a creature of legend.

Haywood turned a fresh page in his notebook. 'Now before we come to how a property owner, landlord and money-lender from Stretford, came to be buried in quicklime under your scullery floor, Mrs. Markham, perhaps you would be kind enough to explain how a governess to the landed gentry came to be acquainted with such a character.'

Elizabeth's gaze travelled round the small, dingy, basement room that served as the inspector's office. Through the window high up beside the ceiling, mud-splattered hems scurried past, spats clicked on the pavement, occasionally a dog would stop to sniff at the glass.

'Mr. Lacey gets his boots hand-made at Norton's,' she explained. 'The establishment supplies Sir Henry and his family with their footwear.'

He snorted. 'Wish I could afford to have my corns and calluses shod there.'

'As, I am sure, do the pit-men of Durham.'

'Hmm.'

That "hmm", she decided, was the "hmm" of a man looking to make Chief Inspector and ultimately Superintendent. Heights unlikely to be scaled, fretting about social concerns. Whereas securing a firm case for the prosecution offered a distinctly promising springboard—

'So it was while ordering a pair of boots for yourself that you encountered William Lacey?'

Elizabeth flashed him a smile that fell midway between sympathetic and wry. 'Like policeman, Inspector, governesses cannot afford bespoke footwear, either.'

Not only poorly paid, they were neither fish nor fowl in the world that they lived in. With a position too elevated to allow them to mix with the servants but too low to join the family, was there ever a colder, lonelier, more miserable existence? For the moment, youth was on Elizabeth's side. But unless she was careful, spinsterhood and poverty were all she had to look forward to, in her old age.

'It was while I was collecting a pair of riding boots for Prudence that I first made Mr. Lacey's acquaintance.'

Ordinarily, Norton's delivered. But it just so happened that Prudence's little fat feet were outstripping their casings faster than you can say knife, to the point where the day dawned where she had a pony saddled and waiting downstairs in the yard, but no boots she could squeeze into.

Now in theory, this being Saturday, it should have been Elizabeth's day off. A day normally spent shoring up contacts, putting out feelers, and generally testing the market for husbands. However, she calculated that if she collected the boots in person, Prudence's tantrums could be calmed in a third of the time, and apart from the pleasure of riding in Sir Henry's carriage, which was not to be sniffed at, with its plumed horses and gold crest on the doors, she would also have an opportunity to gaze into the many shop windows that fronted Bond-street.

That was back in February, of course, and to be frank, very little about that first meeting stood out. She'd been too busy picturing herself swirling around dance floors in the various ball gowns or floating in one of the furs to pay much attention to the portly, rather gingerish, customer with gold-rimmed spectacles perched on the end of his nose. For though his tailoring was impeccable, albeit a tad loud, and his pocket-watch worth a small fortune, Elizabeth was eager to escape her governess life. Not desperate.

The inspector licked the tip of his pencil. 'Yet a friendship between William Lacey and yourself did develop?'

'No impropriety occurred, if that's what you're suggesting.'

'My apologies, Mrs. Markham, for implying anything of the sort.' All the same, he looked disappointed. 'Mr. Lacey may have been no stranger to the law, but his housekeeper vouches most vehemently that she found no, uh, traces of improper conduct on the premises. Indeed, even your husband, who himself seems to be of a passionate and sometimes violent nature, has cast no aspersions on your fidelity.' The gimlet eyes flickered. 'I am simply curious as to what a respectable married woman and an unscrupulous money-lender might have in common.'

Of course he was. The press, too. In fact, the whole world had its tongue hanging out, panting.

For the one thing, there had been no disguising William Lacey's fascination for Elizabeth. In fact, from the moment he stepped aside to allow her to be served before him, he confided to friends how he had been struck by her poise. By the time they were engaged in conversation while Prudence's boots were being attended to, he confessed that her wit and intelligence had him enthralled. Indeed, the instant Elizabeth vacated the premises, Lacey was badgering Mr. Norton about her and then, having discovered where she worked, boasted many times in the weeks that followed of the various "coincidental" meetings that he engineered.

But the police, the public and the jury were no fools. If his attentions had been unwelcome, Elizabeth was more than capable of quashing them. It was obvious as the nose on their face that she had strung him along, but all she would say on the matter was that Mr. Lacey was not husband material.

While making no effort to explain why a renowned drinker and gambler who could not hold a job was.

She shrugged. 'Who can say what binds friendship together, Inspector?'

'Obviously not confidences,' Haywood snapped back. 'Right up until his death, William Lacey remained ignorant in the matter of your marriage, so perhaps you could enlighten me as to why you kept it a secret? Was it that you were ashamed of John Markham?'

'On the contrary.' She smiled demurely. 'I found my husband exciting.'

So did the press. Impoverished spinster living a sheltered life on the one hand. A handsome, cocky, ladies-man on the other. The fact that he was seven years younger than his bride only added to the piquancy of the pairing, and the newspapers left little doubt in their readership's mind that the new Mrs. Markham found her wifely duties less than onerous.

'Then why not tell your "good friend" about your marriage?'

'How cruel you are, Inspector. When I was only too keenly aware of Mr. Lacey's tenderness towards me, why should I desire to hurt his feelings?'

'And this had nothing to do with the fact that Mr. Lacey was of the Roman Catholic persuasion, and that although his wife left him many years previously, he was still legally married?'

'I see absolutely no relevance in the matter.'

Haywood's fist slammed down on the table. 'Mrs. Markham. For broadsheet editors, your composure and beauty might be a front page dream, but a man is dead. Lured to your lodgings in Lexington-place, shot and then buried like litter beneath your kitchen floor, and quicklime thrown over his body. On the very same morning, if you please, that he transferred five thousand pounds' worth of securities into cash, every penny of which has gone missing, while your own husband accuses you of sending him out to purchase an air pistol, a shovel, a bag of quicklime and two train tickets to Brighton. All this, while you yourself were engaged in giving notice to quit your lodgings and selling the bulk of your furniture to a broker, if you please! Oh yes, your husband is also on record as stating that, when he returned home from his walk, he found you in the scullery with blood on your dress, the gun in your hand and the victim dead at your feet.'

His notebook snapped shut.

'Premeditated murder, Mrs. Markham. Now, I grant society has few reasons to mourn William Lacey's passing, but please spare me any pleas about hurting his feelings. The man was killed for a motive as base and pitiless as money, and I have every intention of bringing the perpetrators of this vile crime to justice. So is there anything you wish to say in your defence?' His eyes narrowed at her continued silence. 'Nothing? No questions at all that you wish to ask? Not —' he paused '— not even why the young man who promised so ardently to love, cherish and honour you just three short months ago sold you out?'

Elizabeth drew a deep breath. 'Maybe there is one thing, Inspector.'

'Oh?' He leaned towards her. 'And what might that be?'

'I was wondering if I might have a cup of tea, please? With just half a teaspoonful of sugar?'

· · · ·

IF HER APPROACH INFURIATED the police, then the public was thrilled. So many questions. So few answers.

What happened to the five thousand pounds? There was no trace of it at Lexington-place, and with the house next to a main thoroughfare, half a dozen witnesses were able to confirm that William Lacey was carrying no baggage when he entered the house.

Which begged another question. Where did William Lacey go between cashing in his securities and calling on the Markhams?

And why, if Elizabeth was truly after his fortune, would a woman of such obvious intelligence kill the golden goose before it had laid any eggs?

The prosecution maintained that William Lacey had confided his intentions to liquidate a large amount of capital and that she set out to relieve him of it in the most brutal and callous way. And then, when William Lacey turned up at the house without it, it was claimed that she shot him out of pique — a point the defence were quick to seize on.

Did Mrs. Markham look like a woman who acted out of spite?

The apprehension of the newlyweds at different times and in different locations was also a source of interest and intrigue in the press. They loved the idea of John Markham being run to ground in an hotel in Brighton, then denying all knowledge of the crime. But suddenly switching his story and laying the blame squarely on his wife, once he discovered that she had been apprehended three days afterwards, about to board the boat to Boulogne.

Both prosecution and defence made much of this, as well. Especially since Mrs. Markham openly admitted that she had agreed to meet her husband in Brighton, yet had no intentions of fulfilling that arrangement.

The Crown suggested this was a deliberate attempt on her part to make John the scapegoat for cold-blooded murder.

Her defence counsel quite naturally rejected the allegation, asking the jury whether John Markham struck them as the type who could be bullied into buying shovels, air pistols, quicklime, or indeed any other devices that would obviously lead to murder. He bought these items, they insisted, in order to eliminate the only other contender for his wife's affections. For while Markham did not imagine Elizabeth would violate her marriage vows, he was astute enough to realize that William Lacey was a rich and unrelenting suitor. The motive, they argued, was jealousy, not money. For if, as the Crown alleged, money was at the root of this crime, where was it? Every trunk, suitcase and piece of baggage on the ferry boat had been accounted for, and not one of them contained bulging wads of bank notes.

And of course, all these uncertainties were played out on the front pages of the papers.

What excuse did Elizabeth give William Lacey for leaving her post as a governess?

Was it insecurity on the part of John Albert Markham that eventually drove him to murder?

Was Elizabeth still so besotted with her new and "exciting" husband that she was prepared to cover up the killing of her friend, but not so foolish as to continue to tie herself to the man who had committed such a hideous crime?

Or was it Markham himself who had resolved to kill two birds with one stone, both depriving William Lacey of his money and at the same time securing his wife's affections?

Only two people knew the truth, the editorials contended, and their stories were in conflict. Who was to be believed? The calm and lovely bride, or the arrogant, posturing husband? Perhaps the truth lay somewhere in between, they suggested, and this was nothing more than a classic case of thieves (or in this case, killers) falling out.

Either way, their reporting was utterly without bias, and yet somehow it seemed to reflect public empathy with the lonely spinster approaching her thirtieth birthday, torn between the coarse charisma of John Albert Markham and the steadfast courtship of a wealthy property owner. Strangely, they also reserved some sympathy for Markham, shrewd enough to see that his intelligence did not equal that of either his rival or his wife, that his prospects for work were growing slimmer by the day, and that his animal magnetism was not going to blind Elizabeth to him for ever.

Even William Lacey, for all that he had been shot and buried in an unmarked grave then left to rot, came over as more villain than victim. The press played up his unscrupulous business deals, reported in salacious detail his reputation for evicting widows and orphans, and listed every one of his past brushes with the law, in which only the intervention of smart, expensive lawyers appeared to have kept him out of gaol. The cashing of the securities seemed to simply be a case of bad timing. It wasn't unknown for William Lacey to pay off any persons who had leverage on him, or else use cash to fund business enterprises that could not be traced back to him. Opium trafficking, extortion, vice, protection rackets? These were not unusual trades in Stretford.

Then suddenly everything changed —

CENTRAL CRIMINAL COURT, Oct. 5.
Shortly before 10 o'clock, the jury were brought
from the London Coffee house, where they had once
again spent the night. The judges, Chief Baron
Pettigrew and Mr. Justice Cornwell, accompanied
by the Lord Mayor and Aldermen Keach, Haines and
Webster took their customary seats on the bench and
the prisoners were duly placed at the bar. However,
before the first witness of the day could be summoned,
an event occurred which caused an animation around
the whole of the courtroom.
The Crown produced trial transcripts dating back
nineteen years, which showed that the murder of
William Lacey was identical in almost every respect
to the murder of one Patrick O'Connor, a gauger in

the Customs at the London Docks, who was in
possession of 4,000l. in foreign railway bonds at the time.

The Times. Oct. 6, 1868.

Indeed, the court could only be silenced with cries of "Order, Order!" from the stentorian voice of the usher, when it was shown how Mr. O'Connor's remains were discovered beneath the back-kitchen floor of a house belonging to Frederick and Maria Manning.

Born in Switzerland, they learned how Maria Manning emigrated to Britain, where she worked as a lady's maid to the daughter of the Duchess of Sutherland — and apparently developed a taste for her employer's lifestyle. Indeed, it was while working for Lady Blantyre that she encountered the 50-year-old Irishman, a somewhat unsavoury character by all accounts, who amassed much of his fortune through criminal activities. Maria was attracted to O'Connor, but at the time was also involved with Frederick Manning, a railway guard who almost certainly stole property while employed by the railway, which O'Connor was suspected of fencing. Convinced that Frederick was poised to inherit a large sum of money, Maria chose him as her husband, but when she realised this was nothing but a falsehood, she determined to leave him — taking O'Connor's money with her.

Inviting Patrick O'Connor to dinner, the court heard how she drugged him with laudanum, only to find that he'd invited a friend along that night. Undaunted, she invited him round the following evening with promises of sexual favours, and, when he went to wash his hands, shot him twice in the head. When both bullets failed to kill him, Frederick finished him off with a crowbar, and it appears that Patrick O'Connor's last words as he crossed the kitchen floor to wash his hands were, 'Haven't you finished digging this drain yet?'

Little realising it was his own grave he was stepping over.

CENTRAL CRIMINAL COURT, *Cont'd.*
The court then heard how Mrs. Manning paid
a visit to the deceased's lodgings and calmly
removed everything of value, including his scrip
of foreign railway bonds. She then took a train to

Edinburgh, where she was later arrested trying
to sell Mr. O'Connor's stolen stock.
Frederick was apprehended one week afterwards
in Jersey, at first denying any involvement in the
crime, but later admitting that he had never liked
O'Connor, so he "battered his head in with a
ripping-chisel".

The Times. Oct. 6, 1868.

'This was a cold and calculated crime,' boomed the rich baritone of Mr. Lockhearte, KC, for the Crown.

Tall, distinguished, and with a long pointed nose, his eau-de-cologne carried almost as far as his perfect pronunciation.

'One in which the principal player was equally cold and calculating, and I can offer no better example of Mrs. Manning's character than when the jury returned from their deliberations, which, I might add, was in under forty-five minutes.'

He paused, as all good actors do.

'While delivering their verdict of guilty, Maria Manning began screaming that they had hounded her worse than a wild animal in the forest, and then proceeded to rant at the judge, as he attempted to pass the death sentence.'

Mr. Lockhearte turned slowly towards Elizabeth and made a flourish with his wrist.

'As she was led away to the cells, however, Mrs. Manning straightened her sleeves and was heard, quite distinctly, to enquire of the turnkeys accompanying her how pleasing they had found her performance.'

Seated in her customary corner of the bar, hands folded as was her habit, Elizabeth could feel the hostility of the entire courtroom burning into her. But her face remained expressionless as Mr. Lockhearte continued to address his astonished jury.

'There is no suggestion, gentlemen, that Mrs. Markham was involved in any way in the murder of Patrick O'Connor, since she was merely a child when the incident took place. However!'

Another flourish, this time with papers.

'The Crown is able to furnish proof that she was a resident in the orphanage not one hundred yards from the gaol where the Mannings were hanged, and I submit this newspaper archive in evidence that she cannot possibly claim to have no knowledge of the event.'

THE BERMONDSEY MURDER
EXECUTION OF THE MANNINGS
For five days past, Horsemonger-lane and its
immediate neighbourhood had presented the
appearance of a great fair, so large were the
crowds collected there, and so intense the state
of excitement in which all present appeared to be.
The surrounding beer-shops were crowded.
Windows commanding a view of the scaffold
rose to a Californian price. Above all, there was a
force of 500 police in position on the ground, and
though it is not easy to estimate the number of persons
who were present at the dreadful spectacle, they probably
exceeded 30,000.

The Times. Nov.14, 1849.

'Can it be coincidence,' demanded the faultless vowels of the prosecution, 'that, nineteen years later, Elizabeth Markham née Clarke also conspires to befriend a wealthy, disreputable scoundrel? And that while dangling William Lacey on a string of affection, she sets out to marry a man less intelligent than herself, a drinker in the mould of Frederick Manning, whose greed she, too, can manipulate? Good heavens, how are we to tell one crime apart from the other? Even the escape Mrs. Markham planned for herself is identical. Sending her husband to one destination, while she decamps to another, in exactly the same fashion that Maria Manning intended Frederick to carry the can for the murder of Patrick O'Connor.'

No sympathy in the courtroom. Not an ounce. Not even for John Albert Markham, the cocky young waster now portrayed as a gull. For fool or not, he nevertheless conspired to commit cold-blooded murder — and murder was a capital crime.

'Can there by any doubt,' Mr. Lockhearte demanded of his spellbound audience, 'that Elizabeth Markham spent her intervening years as a governess contemplating the circumstances that surrounded that earlier trial, then set about replicating them to her own ends?'

He ran a finger down the length of his patrician nose, then tapped his lower lip.

'Unfortunately for her, the plan rebounded when Mr. Lacey failed to turn up with the cash as expected. And whilst we will probably never know to what felonious purpose this money has been put, I suggest to you, gentlemen of the jury, that it was greed pure and simple that lay at the heart of this crime.'

You could have heard the proverbial pin drop.

'Mr. Lacey's character has not been portrayed in a good light during this trial. He was a ruthless landlord, who had no qualms about evicting any tenant who did not pay their rent, no matter how desperate or temporary their circumstances, and employed even less patience with those to whom he lent money. His rates of interest have proven to be extortionate, his methods of collection questionable in the extreme, but I must ask you to push these points from your mind.'

No need, they already had.

'Just like the Mannings twenty years earlier, Elizabeth and John Markham have both attempted to pin responsibility for the crime on the other, but it is the Crown's belief, gentlemen, that although Mrs. Markham was the brains behind this scheme, her husband was an all-too-willing partner. Neither, you notice, have uttered a single word of repentance, and it is the Crown's contention that when Mr. Lacey turned up at Lexington-place that fateful morning, he was already aware of Mrs. Markham's plan to rob him. Perhaps he went there to gloat how he had foiled her, perhaps to denounce her, having discovered the truth of her marriage, perhaps even to expose her to the police in a sudden upsurge of Christian spirit.'

Only Lockhearte himself smiled at the joke.

'But I put it to you, gentlemen of the jury, that whatever Mr. Lacey may have said or done that fateful morning, it was compelling enough to motivate the Markhams to silence him once and for all.'

Looking towards the jury, Elizabeth saw the repugnance in their eyes.

And satisfaction in Inspector Haywood's.

CENTRAL CRIMINAL COURT, Oct. 4.
As Mr. Lockhearte, KC, finished summing up the
case for the Crown, Mrs. Markham stood up, walked
across to where her husband was sitting and whispered
something in his ear. Instantly, the constables rushed
forward, but there appeared to be no need for intervention.
By the time they arrived, the female prisoner was seated
facing the bench with her usual composure, while Markham
himself was staring at her with a shocked expression and
his face white.

The Times. Oct. 5, 1868.

And now, twenty-four days after the jury delivered their guilty verdict, Elizabeth sat alone in the dark and the cold, straining for signs of the approaching dawn. Her thoughts fluttered back to when she was nine years old, squashed among the tatterdemalions of London, who had gathered outside Horsemonger-lane gaol — or rather, Surrey County Gaol, as it was called now. Not that the name changed anything. It remained the same bleak, dismal hole, where the ghosts of dead convicts howled on the stairs and the souls of the innocent wept silent tears. And the condemned cells as cold as the grave.

But nineteen years ago, as the night had progressed, the assemblage outside the prison grew denser and more raucous. Elizabeth was able to picture the scene as though it were yesterday. The gaunt outline of the gibbet, dark against even the darkness of the night. The ladder leading up to it. The smoke from the prison's chimneys, even, from fires lit inside to keep the November damp at bay. Long before the sky brightened, she remembered, the windows overlooking the scaffold along Horsemonger-lane were crammed with the gentry. Charles John Huffam Dickens unquestionably among them.

With an imperceptible sigh, she reached for the book at her side and ran the flat of her hand across its open pages. Would Pip ever marry the hideous Estelle—? Softly, very softly, she closed the book and replaced it on the bench.

Great Expectations, indeed...

How curious that her path crossed with Mr. Dickens' all those years ago, neither, of course, having the slightest notion of the impact his influence would have in later years. Yet, as a result of his tireless efforts, only a small group of people would be on hand this morning to witness — to witness —

Elizabeth swallowed. At the time, of course, the spectacle of a husband and wife at the gallows was almost unprecedented, and she couldn't help but wonder what was going through her husband's mind at this dreadful moment. Fourteen years spent in an orphanage, eight as a governess, not to mention watching both parents drown in a boating accident, had left Elizabeth adept at hiding her feelings. No amount of trickery could persuade her to reveal more than she wanted to, but John? For him, too, the seconds would be lumbering past on shackled feet, and he would not be sitting quietly, hands clasped in his lap. Not John. Was he scared, she wondered? Was he down on his knees, praying to his God? Accepting of what the papers referred to the *"awful change"*?

She remembered when Frederick Manning went to the gallows. He wore his best suit, probably his only suit, but what chilled her the most, as she stood there that morning, was the way his shirt-collar had been turned over and loosened, that the rope might be more easily adjusted. She remembered, too, that he'd been shaking so badly that he was unable to mount the scaffold unaided. It had needed a man either side to support him — whereas Maria Manning caused a public sensation. Tying her own black silk handkerchief over her eyes and dressed in a black satin gown, she approached the noose with a firm and unfaltering step. In fact, right up to the end, she remained the consummate performer, and such was the scandal she created, even appealing to Queen Victoria from the condemned cell, that black satin instantly fell out of fashion and had remained that way ever since.

Yet it was neither Frederick's frailty nor Maria's dramatics that inspired Mr. Dickens' campaign.

TO THE EDITOR OF *THE TIMES*
When I came upon the scene at midnight, the
shrillness of the cries and howls that were raised
made my blood run cold. As the night went on,
screeching, and laughing, and parodies on Negro
melodies, with substitutions of "Mrs. Manning"
for "Susannah" were added. When the day dawned,

thieves, low prostitutes, ruffians and vagabonds
flocked to the ground, with every variety of offensive
and foul behaviour. Fightings, faintings, whistlings,
imitations of Punch, brutal jokes, tumultuous
demonstrations of indecent delight when swooning
women were dragged out of the crowd by the police
with their dresses disordered, gave a new zest to the
general entertainment.
When the sun rose brightly—as it did—it gilded
thousands upon thousands of upturned faces, so
inexpressibly odious in their brutal mirth that a man
had cause to feel ashamed of the shape he wore, and
to shrink from himself, as fashioned in the image of the
Devil.
When the two miserable creatures who attracted
all this ghastly sight were turned quivering into the air,
there was no more emotion, no more pity, no more
thought that two immortal souls had gone to judgment,
than if the name of Christ had never been heard in this
world.

Charles Dickens.
Devonshire-Terrace. Tuesday, Nov 13.

The prosecution was quite correct in its supposition. Elizabeth's had indeed been one of those gilded upturned faces, and long after Frederick and Maria Manning were cut down and the crowd dispersed, she had remained transfixed beneath the prison gates.

After first denying any knowledge of Patrick O'Connor's body beneath his kitchen floor, then blaming his wife for everything, Frederick finally made his confession to his brother. Even to admitting that he had dug the grave one month in advance of O'Connor's death.

Maria, on the other hand, demonstrated the same firmness of character that she had shown from the beginning and indeed right throughout her trial. She went to her grave, taking all her secrets with her.

As Elizabeth herself would.

. . . .

'WHY, MR. LACEY, WHAT a coincidence. This must be the third weekend running that we have bumped into one other!'

Coincidence be damned, and it also was the fourth time that she had encountered him. The first occasion, of course, she'd dismissed as pure chance. Then she noticed the glint in his eye. The same glint Sir Henry Wilton used to get when a rare Eastern treasure came on the antiquities market, which meant he wouldn't rest until he had added it to his collection. Like all collectors, Sir Henry was obsessive and Elizabeth recognised the trait in William Lacey at once.

'Upon my soul Mr. Lacey, I do believe you have grown a set of mandy whiskers since last I saw you.'

He made an expansive gesture with his hands. 'I cannot deny it.'

Elizabeth stepped back to admire what was still little more than stubble. 'I do declare, whiskers make you quite handsome, Mr. Lacey.'

He gave her that sly, sideways smile from beneath his ginger lashes that somehow made her skin crawl.

'Not handsome, Miss Clarke.'

With a body that had grown pudgy from too much rich food and too little exercise and skin that was waxy from too much time spent indoors, William Lacey was fully aware of his physical shortcomings. Just as he was conscious of his assets.

'Never handsome, I think.'

He wound his ridiculously expensive timepiece, to prove the point.

Elizabeth's smile was wry. 'Distinguished, then.'

He adjusted his gold-rimmed spectacles. 'Might I buy you a cream tea, Miss Clarke?'

And so it was, over scones and jam and clotted cream, that the dance began. Elizabeth was no fool. In certain circles, for a woman to remain unmarried when she was approaching thirty was the ultimate humiliation. But a governess, being neither fish nor fowl, fell into no such category, and she, too, knew her worth. She had no money, no prospects, and although she made the most of her appearance and lacked neither wit nor intelligence, there were plenty with more to offer.

Except men are men.

They all want to melt the Ice Queen...

'It is unfortunate, Miss Clarke, that I was forced to evict a widow, a toddler and her baby from that very house on Wednesday.'

Cream teas had grown into long walks, dinners, picnics, carriage rides. He particularly liked to show her the properties he owned in Shoreditch, Mile End, Stretford, Stepney, and would always let drop the amount he raked in from rents and what he liked to describe as "other enterprises".

'Number 19, at the end there, is currently leased at three times the customary rate.' His tongue flickered over his thick, pink lips. 'The gentleman in question is being sought by the police, although he assures me it is a misunderstanding and that he is completely innocent. Naturally, I would not rent to him otherwise.'

'Naturally.'

And so the dance moved on, with both partners keeping smoothly in step with William Lacey continuing to promote his wealth and Elizabeth remaining out of reach. It was exactly as she told Inspector Haywood in her statement. No impropriety took place. But the situation could not continue for ever, and it came to a head at the end of September.

'The orphans you threw in the street, Mr. Lacey. Do you not fear for their future?'

More tea, more cakes. Elizabeth did not think she would eat another scone again.

'It is a very different future I am preparing, Miss Clarke.' He shot her his strange, sideways glance. 'The increase I will be able to obtain from the next tenant will add towards a very comfortable retirement.'

Elizabeth folded her hands on the table. 'You are a long way from retirement age, I think, Mr. Lacey.'

Another sly glance. 'With the right financial background, a man can retire to the country earlier than one might otherwise have expected.' He cleared his throat. 'I'm told two can live as cheaply as one there.'

At long last the dance was at an end —

'You seem to forget that you are still married, Mr. Lacey.'

'Technically speaking, Miss Clarke. But in the, uh, country, folk may not always be privy to the full details of a person's marital status. If you take my meaning.'

A bogus marriage? And what would she get out of it, if he died? He could change his will at any moment without her knowing, and she wouldn't have a leg to stand on and Elizabeth knew all about collectors. It wasn't that they didn't cherish what they had. But the pleasure of ownership didn't compare with the excitement of chasing after something new.

Elizabeth leaned across the table and smiled from under lowered lashes.

'I have always enjoyed the country, Mr. Lacey.'

And before he could say anything in reply, the bell in the tea-shop was tinkling at her departure, and by the time he had settled the bill, she was out of sight.

A week passed, a week in which she did not reply to any of his notes. Notes which arrived every day, sometimes twice, and which she burned immediately. Especially since the address was still Sir Henry's.

'Thank you.'

She gave the boy who intercepted them his usual farthing, and ten days after their last meeting, set off for Stretford, knowing full well that William Lacey would be at home, going through his accounts, as he did every Thursday afternoon.

'Miss Clarke! Elizabeth!' His surprise was unambiguous, his delight genuine. 'Come in.'

As he poured them both a glass of sherry, there was no reference to his recent blizzard of letters, no mention of the proposition made across a plate of Eccles cakes. Instead, he tried to kiss her.

She pushed him away with a firmness that surprised him. And a new dance began.

'You do not find me attractive, do you?' he asked at length.

'No, sir, I do not.'

'No.' He nodded slowly. Sipped the remainder of his sherry. Then stood up, walked across the room and unlocked the top drawer of his bureau. 'But you find these attractive, I suspect. Securities, madam. Five thousand pounds in this sheaf alone.' He pursed his lips. 'Now don't tell me you don't find *that* attractive.'

As she stared at the bundle of papers tied up with red string, Elizabeth knew there could be no more beating around the bush. For either of them.

She drew a deep breath. Looked him squarely in the eye.

'The honest truth, Mr. Lacey? The honest truth is that those things mean nothing to me, nothing at all.'

She paused, then walked across to stand so close to him that her breath misted up the lenses of his spectacles..

'But if you were to turn those securities into twenty pound notes and spread them over the bed in the honeymoon suite of the Claybourne Hotel in the name of Mr. & Mrs. John Smith—' She blew softly in his ear. 'Why, William, I would be yours to command.'

Breezing out without a backward glance, she tried to dispel the notion of his oily little body pounding up and down on hers. Surely that was the most repugnant prospect in the world, but after five months, Elizabeth knew William Lacey inside out. She knew he would not hesitate to cash in those securities. Just as she knew he would not hesitate to buy them back the following day!

But one step at a time...

For not once, since standing beneath that gaunt, dark gibbet in Horsemonger-lane, had she forgotten Maria Manning. Maria Manning had also grown used to a life in which the beds were soft, the rooms were warm, there was sufficient money to pay for both food and fuel. Maria the lady's maid wanted that for the rest of her life, as did Elizabeth, the governess, and hearing about the widows and orphans who were thrown into the street only hardened her resolve against being in thrall to landlords like William Lacey.

The trouble was, Maria Manning was greedy. If she hadn't tried to sell Patrick O'Connor's railway stocks so soon afterwards, if she hadn't kept his valuables to sell on later, indeed if she hadn't tried to have her cake and eat it, in all probability she would have got away with it.

And Elizabeth had had twenty years to learn from Maria's mistakes...

Drawing on all those Saturdays spent shoring up contacts, putting out feelers and generally testing the market for husbands, she decided John Albert Markham was the best man to take that long walk down the aisle. He drank, he gambled, he bragged and he was lazy, but equally he was handsome, strong and funny, and the marriage bed was hardly an ordeal. Crucially, John Albert

Markham was infatuated. He, too, had a passionate desire to melt the Ice Queen and was young enough, and not quite bright enough, to believe that the attraction of opposites would last. Most importantly, however, John was no collector. He was a simple soul who lived on debt in rented lodgings, yet saw a future in which he and Elizabeth raised children, grandchildren, lived and died together. And because he was a gambling man, he had no realistic vision of what financial threads might sow this miracle together.

But understood exactly what five thousand pounds could do —

Taking her cue from Maria, Elizabeth brought her husband into her plan. And like Frederick Manning twenty years before him, John was a willing partner.

'You're sure he'll bring the money to the house?'

'Absolutely certain,' she assured him, with a kiss. 'Trust me.'

And so, just like Maria Manning, Elizabeth lured William Lacey to Lexington-place (she claimed it was a friend's house), shot him in the same manner as the Mannings had killed O'Connor, with an air pistol (although thankfully, the first bullet killed him outright, the second was simply a precaution) and together she and John buried William Lacey in the quick-lime purchased by her husband, just like the Mannings had before them. In fact, so famous was the trial that the prosecution couldn't fail to pick up on the similarities, but if Maria could so easily have escaped arrest, how was it that Elizabeth got caught?

'No matter how intelligent murderers think they are,' thundered Mr. Lockhearte for the Crown, 'they always make that one mistake.'

He had turned and stared directly to where Elizabeth Markham was sitting, and she saw the triumph in his eyes.

'That one mistake that allows us to claim justice for the victim.'

• • • •

WITH A JOLT OF SURPRISE, Elizabeth saw that the sky was changing colour. The dawn, which had been so long in coming, had suddenly arrived, pink, and streaked with grey.

With a deep, shuddering breath she adjusted the fringe of black lace that almost, but not quite, covered her eyes. In her mind she had lived this moment a thousand, two thousand times. The chaplain's pious murmurs. The pinioning of the hands. The long walk down the passageways fenced in with gates and side rails. Stepping over the condemned prisoner's own gaping grave.

From somewhere a male voice intruded on the horror. 'It's time now, Miss.'

Time. What did time mean, when a white cap was about to be placed over one's head and a noose fitted round one's neck?

'Thankfully, I shall never know,' she whispered to herself, collecting her gloves and reticule.

Through the tiny aperture that passed for a window on this little ferry boat, the lights of the ocean-going liner that would carry her across the Atlantic loomed into view.

New York. New World. New life…

CENTRAL CRIMINAL COURT, Oct. 4.
It was not the fact that Mrs. Markham suddenly
got up and whispered to her husband, however,
that caused excitement round the courtroom.
It was because, shortly after she had re-seated
herself, Markham jumped out of his own chair
and shouted "Very well, I confess! It <u>was</u> me!
I shot William Lacey with the pistol that I
procured for the purpose. My wife is as innocent
of this crime as she claims!"

The Times. Oct. 5, 1868.

Do they, Mr. Lockhearte? Do all murderers make that one mistake? To be caught waiting to board that boat to Boulogne had been part of Elizabeth's plan. Standing trial was key to it, as well. For, once acquitted, no person may be tried twice for murder. Double jeopardy is not recognised in law.

She picked up the book, whose ending she would never know. Or rather would never care to know. In these past twenty-four days, when all she'd had to do was read and wait and wait and read, she'd had enough Dickens to last her for a lifetime. But what else could she do? It was always possible that John Albert Markham might receive a pardon, or that the truth would somehow come tumbling out.

But now, at the time the prison bell would be tolling and the public executioner positioning her husband over the trapdoor, Elizabeth saw that Mr. Lockhearte was quite wrong. With twenty years to learn from Maria Manning's mistakes, she had learned her lessons well.

'Mr. & Mrs. John Smith?' William Lacey had murmured.

'If I am to give myself to you on a bed of twenty pound notes, I would prefer to retain at least some small modicum of pride,' she replied, with eyes oh-so-demurely downcast.

And there it was. At ten o'clock precisely, William Lacey liquidated five thousand pounds of securities into cash at his bank in Bloomsbury and carried the suitcase ... straight across the road to the Claybourne Hotel. He obviously made no connection between his bank and the hotel she had chosen. It was, after all, second only to the Ritz. But Elizabeth needed to be sure there was no trail for the police to follow. And who would suspect William Lacey would simply carry his cash over the road?

She watched him leave the hotel after twenty minutes or so. She already had a hackney standing, so that even as the doorman was hailing him a cab, she was already on her way, ahead of him. Having spun her tale of running out on Sir Henry and using her friend's house as a hiding place, she waited. And then, once the body was buried and John on the train to Brighton, a rather tarty looking Mrs. Smith checked into the Bridal Suite, gathered up the bank notes spread across the bed, packed them back in the suitcase, settled the account and deposited the trunk in the Left Luggage Office at Victoria Station.

As Mrs. Markham once again, she booked a passage to Boulogne and calmly waited while the alarm was raised and the body found. And what foresight, to send a note to his house after he had left that fateful morning, to make sure the interval would not be long! Then, it was simply a question of waiting.

Waiting to be arrested.

Waiting to be tried.

Waiting for John Albert Markham to bear full responsibility for the crime.

Waiting to claim the trunk of money.

Waiting for this dawn, when the only other person who knew the truth would now be dead...

For days after her acquittal, the newspapers had been brimming with speculation about this astonishing reversal of events. What, they goggled, had Mrs. Markham whispered to her husband? What could *possibly* be of such great importance that he instantly changed his plea to guilty?

Oh, what fools men are!

'I'm pregnant, John.' She patted the black satin gown that had also attracted so much attention in the press. 'I'm carrying your child.'

It was all the spur he'd needed. The thought of his name, his very bloodline, dying out, when all he had ever wanted was a family was too much for John to bear. He would rather go to his death shouldering the blame than kill his only child.

As Elizabeth knew he would.

And poor, simple, trusting John. Did no one tell him that they don't hang pregnant women?

Ascending the gangplank, dwarfed by the giant liner overhead, Elizabeth dropped her copy of *Great Expectations* into waters turned scarlet with the breaking sky. Never mind Pip's chances of marriage to the vile Estelle. Once in America, and with five thousand pounds behind her, Elizabeth did not think it long before she became a wife again herself.

Or a widow, come to that.

With its golden sands, rugged cliffs and stout stone piers, Lisscombe was about as picture perfect as any cove on the north Devonshire coast. Colourful fishing boats bobbed safely in the the harbour. Nets and crab traps lined the quay. Thatched cottages stood guard, as they had for centuries.

'B-lisscombe,' the Tourist Board billed it, with the slogan *Stay for a week, remember for a lifetime.*

Groovy, babe. They'd remember this week, with Ruth top of the list, because that's the trouble with thatched cottages. Those walls would happily withstand another few centuries, but once the roof catches fire, there's no stopping it. Three hundred year-old wooden beams plus a twelve inch layer of dry straw equals flames to the moon, heat fiercer than Dante's *Inferno,* and a pall of smoke you can see for ten miles. A spectacle which the whole village had turned out to watch, and why not? The tourist season didn't start for a fortnight.

Humming *Ruby Tuesday* to take her mind off the climb—steep hills being thin on the ground in London—Ruth wheezed her way to the source of the buzz.

Yesterday, the cottage was a postcard producer's dream, clinging to the cliff edge, all whitewashed walls, roses round the door and the sea sparkling in the background. Today it was the fire brigade's worst nightmare.

Blimey. Looking at the grungy crimplene frocks and clodhopping flatties, the Summer of Love had sure given Lisscombe a wide body swerve. The words psych and delic weren't tripping off anyone's tongues here, just as no one here was tripping, full stop. But that chick? The one making squiggles in a spiral bound notebook? She'd got the memo for sure. Dig those spider false eyelashes and flick-ups. That was hip, man, outta sight, ditto the chain belt and white go-go boots. Mind, she also had the sort of curves that made Ruth wish she'd stuffed more padding in her bra before she left this morning, but still. Ruth wriggled through to where the chick was making notes. If anyone gets the low-down on what's going on, it's a journo.

'This is my property.' The owner of the cottage, who also happened to be the architect of the blaze, wasn't shouting. Even so, her voice carried pitch perfect

above the wail of sirens, clatter of ladders, and the crackle and snap of reeds being consumed by the flames. *'I can do what I like with it.'*

An argument which seemed perfectly valid to her, but held little sway with the army of firemen risking their lungs and their lives to control the bloody thing.

'Not your average arsonist, then?' the reporter asked no one in particular.

Ain't that the truth, Ruth thought. Not that she had any experience with the species, but then, she hadn't imagined them looking like Audrey Hepburn in *Breakfast at Tiffany's*, either. Right down to the cigarette holder, chignon, and strappy cocktail dress at—she checked her watch—ten thirty-five in the morning.

'Honest to Moses,' tutted a woman in an old-fashioned wrap-around apron. 'The whisky industry would have gone out of business years ago, if it wasn't for that Suzanne Cinq-Mars.'

'Be fair,' someone else said, 'the life she's led would drive any girl to drink.'

'Girl?' Mrs. Apron rolled her eyes. 'If that woman's the bright side of fifty, I'm a Dutchman.'

Tugging at her mini skirt, Ruth adjusted her sunglasses and stood on tiptoe for a better look. Not at the flashing lights and furious unfurling of hoses, or even the wall of fuzz struggling to hold back the crowd. Her interest lay in the willowy, vaguely feline creature at the centre of this mid-morning, midsummer drama.

'Still behaves like the singing sensation she thought she was in the War,' sneered a woman wearing curlers held in place by a hairnet. 'Please note the word "thought".'

'May I remind you, gentlemen, this is private property.' The world's most elegant arsonist had already locked the front door and thrown the key in the flames. *'You have no right to enter without my permission.'*

The brigade chief, distinguishable by the only white helmet among a sea of black, bypassed trying to reason with her. He yanked her out of the way with one hand, while the other motioned two of his crew forward, wet cloths covering their mouths, to take their axes to the door. Solid oak, the damn thing didn't budge.

'I saw her perform once.' Mrs. Apron lit a cigarette, which seemed somewhat ironic under the circs. 'Suzanne Cinq-Mars indeed. What sort of a name is that?'

'Stripper's name, if you ask me.' Mrs. Hairnet sniffed.

'During the War.' Mrs. Apron turned to the reporter. 'When I was in the WAAF and stationed up in Blackpool, a few of us girls hit the town one night, and dear oh dearie me. Listening to your Elvis, your Rolling Stones, your Kinks today, you'd think sex was only invented in 1958. Well, they didn't see Suzanne Cinq-Mars in the Paradise Club.' She took a long pull on her ciggie. 'Poured into a peach satin evening gown, she was, trying to look like she was nude, and making the most suggestive movements you could imagine.' She lowered her voice to a comical whisper. 'Rumour has it the *Boogie Woogie Bugle Boy from Company B* was never the same after that.'

'If only she'd stuck to bugles,' Mrs. Hairnet said. 'Or boys.'

'Never trust a trumpet player.'

'I thought you said he played the trombone. Or was it the sax?'

'He played the field, love, I know that. Married man, as well. Dropped her like a brick, when she told him she was pregnant. Flat out denied the kid was his.'

'Rough luck, though.' Mrs. Hairnet pulled a face. 'Two bright young things with the world at their feet, yet before you can say Benny Goodman, one's lumbered with a kiddie and no financial support, while the other's gone on to join a top swing band, and touring the world.'

'You say that, but at least she got a house out of it.' Mrs. Apron turned to the reporter. 'Inherited that cottage after her uncle died in '42.'

'El Alamein?'

'Heart attack.' Mrs. Apron dabbed her eyes with a suprisingly delicate lace-trimmed hankie. 'Ask me, it was the stress of taking in his neice. Suzanne's parents having thrown her out, on account of the kid being the wrong side of the blanket.'

'God knows what I'd have done, if my parents disowned me,' a plump young worman in a red cardigan chipped in. 'But between you and me, I'm betting Miss Sophistication over there, used to the high life and whooping it up, felt seriously shortchanged. And at the peak of her career, as well.'

'I know exactly what her reaction was!' Mrs. Hairnet sniffed in derision. 'Twice, not once, *twice* she tried to get rid of that baby.'

'For heaven's sake,' Red Cardi said, 'how would anyone know that?'

'Mrs. Bellamy, who worked in the chemist's, said that's what set her off on the booze. Backstreet jobs both times, she said, right botch-ups, and whisky's well known in those circles for easing the pain.' She nudged the reporter with her elbow. 'Not just those circles. Twice a week I pretend I've got a migraine, just to cure it.'

Unreal, man. Un-bloody-real. A life-threatening drama's playing out fifty yards away, and this lot are putting on a three-dog comedy show! Mind you, who wasn't? As much as the crowd pretended to be torn between terror and outrage, without exception they were dishing up the same salacious mix of rumour, slander, gossip and hearsay. Which the cool reporter with the spider lashes and go-go boots was recording verbatim.

'Go away, please, I have work to do.'

To prove her point, the owner of the cottage tossed a Molotov cocktail on to the roof. The crowd gasped from the extra surge of heat, but not a single soul moved back. The reporter's pencil filled another page.

'I don't believe a word about those backstreet abortions.' Red Cardi craned her neck for a better view. 'Suzanne's a recluse to her marrow, and considering she's barely exchanged two words with the milkman in the twenty years she's lived here, how can anyone know she tried to smother her baby?'

'Seriously?' Ruth couldn't help herself. 'Suffocate her own daughter?'

Mrs. Apron ground her cigarette butt under her heel and nodded grimly. 'Nellie Harrod—lived above the ironmonger's—told me hand on heart, God rest her soul, how she popped round one morning to borrow a cup of sugar, and found Suzanne Cinq-Mars in the garden, leaning over the pram with a blanket pressed over the poor little mite's mouth.'

Red Cardi snorted. 'Why didn't she report it to the police, then?'

'It was only years later, Nellie said, when those other accusations began to surface, that she started to doubt Suzanne's explanation. That maybe it wasn't sick she was wiping up after all.'

Ruth's eyes followed the human chain, passing buckets like there was no tomorrow and barely flinching from the heat of the crackling flames. At the front of the crowd, an old lady with a dowager's hump was being helped into an ambulance, blood streaming from her face after tripping over a rock. Someone had brought a transistor radio to help pass the time, someone else took a photo, quite a few were passing bags of sweets around, and in the midst of all this drama?

Suzanne Cinq-Mars.

Glamorous, drunk, self-absorbed, calm, playing to a crowd she took great pains to ignore.

'What accusations?' the reporter asked, sharpening her pencil.

'That rumour about the kiddie in the bath, for one.' Red Cardi crossed her arms across breasts in dire need of decent support, and Ruth didn't understand. She just really didn't dig it. Beneath the frumpy clothes and mumsy hair was a girl what—six? seven years older than herself. How could someone that young let themselves go? 'But that was malice, pure and simple.'

'Don't be so quick to judge, love.' Mrs. Apron wagged her finger. 'Mrs. Osborne—worked in the haberdasher's, you're too young to remember her—she knocked to deliver some ribbon Suzanne ordered. Peered through the window, saw Miss High and Mighty curled up on the sofa reading *Vogue*, and when she asked about the little girl, that's when Suzanne told her she was upstairs in the bath. Well, you've got kiddies, Alison Bunce. Would *you* leave a two-year-old alone in water?'

'You're right,' Red Cardi said, 'I don't remember Mrs. Osborne, but according to my mum, who went to school with her, she was a mischief making rhymes-with-witch, and since Suzanne's baby didn't drown, we only have Mrs. O's word for it. Which, quite frankly, I wouldn't trust an inch.'

'What about the bruises, then?'

'Come on, Joanie, my boys fall out of trees like apples. Does that make me a bad mother?'

'We know she pushed her daughter down the stairs? There's no denying that. Poor mite ended up in hospital with two cracked ribs, a broken collar bone and a dislocated knee, not to mention a twisted hand that never did straighten properly again.'

Ruth suppressed a shudder and instinctively flexed her fingers.

'Wouldn't the hospital have pressed further, if they thought there was something sinister behind it?' she asked, hoping the reporter wouldn't mind someone else muscling in.

'Of *course* the hospital took it further,' Mrs. Apron said irritably. 'But I tell you, that Suzanne's nothing if not plausible. Passed it off with how all kiddies lark about, they trip, and sometimes, yes, they hurt themselves. Claimed it was all part of growing up, and for their sins, the authorities believed her.'

'Why didn't you?' Ruth was curious.

'Well, for one thing, Suzanne wasn't the sort to let her daughter run wild, and for another, I never saw an ounce of love go into that kiddie. Not one, poor little mite.'

Red Cardi snorted. 'None of us knows what goes on behind closed doors, Joan.'

Especially, thought Ruth, when they're as heavy as the one the firemen were trying to break down, and your house walls are eighteen bleedin' inches thick.

'That's my point, love, who *does* know what goes on? All I can say is, there were too many rumours going round for my liking, too many visits by the school inspectors, and to this day, I still remember Suzanne calling up the street to Mrs. Osbourne, *if I'm such a terrible mother, why don't they take my daughter into care?*'

'Joanie, if they thought the girl was at risk, they would have.'

'You're forgetting, this was end-of-War, love. There wasn't any Social Services in those days, no National Health...' For the second time, Mrs. Apron wiped her eyes, and again, it wasn't from the smoke. 'All we had was a sodding awful mess to clear up, and a stack of fresh graves in the churchyard. Honest to Moses, peace was ten times worse than the War.'

'How so?' Ruth asked.

'With no enemy to fight, and no one to hate any more, peace was a right old anti-climax. Left a monstrous black hole in our lives and our hearts, it did, and for a long time we had nothing to fill it with. Especially us women, forced to give up our independence and go back to the kitchen like the submissive little creatures we're told we are. But.' She blew her nose defiantly. 'Life goes on, don't it? You roll up your sleeves and bloody well get on with it, because what choice do you have?'

Growing up through the Bill Haley, Chuck Berry, Buddy Holly era, and now the Swingin' Sixties, all love and weed and peace, man, ban the bomb, Ruth was suddenly ashamed that she'd taken progress not only for granted, but that, in her eyes, student protests, hot pants and Woodstock were natural building blocks in the construction of this exciting new future. It never crossed her mind that women like Mrs. Apron—and there were millions of them—had already tasted this kind of freedom.

Before the rug was snatched from under them.

'As for Suzanne and that poor kiddie,' Mrs. Hairnet was saying, 'there's no smoke without fire, pun most definitely intended. In fact, it was on account of the mother not loving her that the nipper ran away, and her only ten years old, as well.'

'My mum told me,' Red Cardi said, 'that, at the time, you thought Suzanne had done away with the girl.'

'What cheek! Mrs. Stephens went round saying that, not me. Remind me to have a word with your mother, next time I see her.'

From the tinny transistor radio, Scott McKenzie was urging everyone going to San Francisco to wear flowers in their hair. Ruth decided she'd quite like to go to San Francisco. Tune in, turn on, drop out, all sex 'n' drugs and rock 'n' roll. She bet it wasn't a patch on this, though.

'You wouldn't believe the rumours flying round when Suzanne's daughter went away,' Red Cardi told the reporter. 'By then, I'd left school two, three, maybe even four years, because that's how it is in places like this. No chance of university, especially us girls.'

At fifteen, she explained, you were out of school and on your own. Leastways, until you found yourself a husband.

And immediatedly Ruth slammed her conclusions about pudding basin haircuts and frumpy blouses in reverse. Christ, it wasn't so much that Red Cardi had let herself go. More that she hadn't let herself start. You grow up, you marry, have kids, so if life's mapped out in advance like a military campaign, why bother?

Ruth's stomach twisted.

Why? Because without making that effort, without putting up a fight, Mrs. Apron's generation sacrificed their freedom for nothing.

And the transistor radio turned to A Whiter Shade of Pale.

'Anyway, it was summer,' Red Cardi was saying. 'I was waitressing in what used to be *Rosebud Cottage* tea rooms before it changed its name to *Strawberry Fayre,* and honestly, you've never heard so many wacky theories in your life.'

'At the time it wasn't funny.' Mrs. Apron chuckled anyway. 'But she's right, talk about speculation. Depending on who you spoke to, the daughter was—' she ticked them off on her work-roughened fingers '—the victim of a serial killer, although of course we didn't call 'em that in them days. Kidnapped by Arabs for the white slave trade. Ran off to join the circus—'

'Or the gypsies.'

'Committed suicide—'

'—which her mother then hushed up.'

'Honest to Moses, love, the list was endless. You couldn't make it up.'

Mrs. Hairnet was not the type to be outdone. 'I heard for a fact she went to Hollywood. Starstruck, after some famous film star spent a week here on his holidays.'

'Famous film star, my sit-upon.' Mrs. Apron snorted. '*His* only claim to fame was appearing alongside Peter O'Toole in a stage play as an extra, and honestly, dear. Do you really see a caravan's footlights turning a young girl's head?'

'She had to have been more than ten when she left,' Red Cardi said pensively. 'My first job was in the Co-op, on the cheese and bacon counter. After that I worked in the sweet shop for a year, then—'

With a splintering crash, the door surrendered to the firemen's axes. Wiping the soot and sweat from their eyes, the exhausted crew stepped aside for their colleagues.

Funny thing, Ruth thought. In a couple of weeks, once the schools had broken up, shops that were boarded up a hundred and fifty feet below would be spilling over with shrimp nets and swimsuits, buckets and spades, and sticks of bright pink, tooth-cracking rock. Now-empty pavements would once again turn into obstacle courses of ice cream carts, postcard racks and wire baskets bursting with beach balls and water wings, while every third lamp post would be plastered with adverts for donkey rides on the sands, deckchairs for hire, or listing the performance times for Punch & Judy shows on the beach. Of course, the fishing boats would still be bobbing in and out of the harbour to the same old rhythm of the tide. But childish squeals would be drowning out the screech of seagulls, the sky would be dotted with puffs of white clouds instead of plumes of black smoke—and today's drama would be wrapped round fish and chips.

'You have no right!'

'We need to make sure there's no one inside, Miss Cinq-Mars, you know that.'

Ruth was reduced to lip reading the fire chief's words, because the only voice that carried above the crackle, shouts and hissing from the hoses was the arsonist's, and let's face it. It doesn't matter how far a mind's lost to Haig and Johnny Walker. A classically trained singer always has good lungs.

'You're wasting your time, there's no one inside.'

'THERE'S SOMEONE INSIDE!'

The crowd sobered instantly.

The crew in the doorway waved for reinforcements.

Ruth felt a chill run through to her marrow.

'Oh, dear God.' Mrs. Apron was gasping, quite literally, for breath. 'Not Lorelei, please God, not little Lorelei!'

'That's the daughter,' Red Cardi said thickly, patting her friend on the back. 'Suzanne got a letter from her only last week, saying she was coming to visit, that's how we know she wasn't done away with all those years ago.'

'Her what chars for the Post Office saw it,' Mrs. Hairnet said. 'The envelope was torn, but she could still read the first few lines and that's how everyone knew Lorelei was coming.'

Ruth's heart was thumping, she barely heard. A fire's one thing. Given the drama of the inferno followed by an arsonist behaving like the star of a black and white movie, you can forgive all this frivolity and gossip where the figures don't add up. Here was a hot house orchid transplanted in to a village of hardy perennials, and the conundrum of the missing child had been niggling away for years. Hell, yeah. Because for all the inconsistencies—one minute Suzanne's arriving in 1942, the next she's only lived here twenty years, and why weren't the police involved, if there was even a *sniff* of crime—the little girl's fate would have preyed on their conscience.

Fishing villages are close-knit communities. Suzanne was an outsider, who kept more than the average distance. This clash of cultures created the perfect breeding ground for Chinese whispers, but now, at last, the community had the chance to air the unease that they'd kept to themselves for so long. And how better, than watching the object of their misgivings setting fire to her own house? Not so much gossip, more communal soul searching.

Should they have tried harder?

Could they have done more?

But passing round bags of barley sugar while pointing the finger firmly at the mother was one thing. Especially now some busybody had breached the confidentiality of the Royal Mail to broadcast Lorelei's return.

'You do know that's illegal?' the reporter was saying.

'Gosh, yes,' Red Cardi said. 'The post master sacked her on the spot.'

'The police were called, too,' Mrs. Apron said firmly. 'But it didn't stop the nosey cow repeating what she'd read.'

And so, tapping their feet to how one pill makes you big, and one pill makes you small, but the ones your mother gives you, don't do anything at all, the people of Lisscombe gathered on the clifftop to watch the flames and stuff their mouths with peppermint lumps, cheerfully absolving themselves of blame, while the breeze carried any residue of guilt out to sea on the pall of black smoke.

Until three words threw off the balance.

Until the fireman said, 'There's someone inside...'

Suddenly, they were not so sure. Not so sure of Suzanne. Not so sure of themselves. Not so sure anyone could survive that inferno, and for God's sake, who could it be? The answer wasn't rocket science. Suzanne never had guests. The person locked inside was Lorelei.

What brought her back after all these years? Why now? What happened? What changed? Theories buzzed like angry bees. Did mother and daughter quarrel? Had Suzanne hit her in a drunken rage and, when the girl fell, Lorelei accidentally hit her head? Or had Suzanne finally tipped over the edge and murdered the child she'd tried to kill so many times, so very long ago..?

Everyone climbed this cliff this morning, expecting a performance.

No one expected a victim.

Now faces paled. Stomachs lurched. Hands were clamped over mouths. You could see their minds working, because deep inside they wondered—no, they *knew*—they could have prevented this tragedy. Dammit, they should have *forced* Suzanne to fit in. They should have dragged her along to join the WI, the PTA, all the other boring institutions they hated being part of, but hell, that's what you do in tiny communities. You pitch in. Sure, you might embellish stories, sure, you might make them up, but at the end of the day, you're a team and you all have each other's back. Except Lorelei's...

And now Ruth's own fists were clenched, her stomach tight, and she knew, if she looked at the mirror in her compact, that her face would be as pale as any white-washed cottage wall. The reason for her anxiety? Suzanne Cinq-Mars, who else? Because, despite being held back by a blank-faced policeman, she was calmly blowing smoke rings, looking like she hadn't a care in the world....

A ripple ran round the crowd.

'*Quick!*'

'*Look!*'

'*They're bringing out the victim.*'

Ruth's heart stopped.

'Hail Mary, Mother of God.' Mrs. Apron crossed herself. 'I can't look. I can't bear it.' She spoke for everyone. 'Is the girl alive?'

Ruth knew even less about corpses than she did about arsonists. On the other hand, you didn't need medical training to see that what the fireman carried over his shoulder was a dressmaker's dummy.

Inappropriate or not, she burst out laughing.

• • • •

FOUR YEARS EARLIER, Dr. Beeching set about streamlining British Rail by closing over half the stations and axeing a third of the routes. Not a single soul in Lisscombe—except perhaps the vicar, who'd find the silver lining in an outbreak of bubonic plague—expected the town to escape the cuts, but for some reason, it was spared. Perhaps it was on account of the mackerel, pollock, plaice and crab that was landed with the tide before heading off to restaurants in London. Perhaps it was because Butlins, Pontins, or one of the other big holiday camp chains had its eye on this pretty little cove, and the Government weighed line closures against the income generated from B-lisscombe becoming the Glamorous Granny and Knobbly Knee capital of North Devon. Perhaps the branch line was simply so small that no one even noticed it was there. Who knows? One thing was sure, though. The afternoon train to London rarely saw a passenger out of season, so imagine Ruth's surprise at find herself sharing the carriage with two other women.

'Read that again, please. That piece about the castle.'

Gone was the strappy cocktail dress, covered in debris and reeking of smoke. In its place, Suzanne wore a tailored suit and starched white shirt straight out of the '40s. More Katherine Hepburn now, than Audrey. Still every inch the star.

The reporter, equally hip, having changed into a sleeveless orange dress emblazoned with swirling purple, green and white circles, leafed through her notes.

'*Picture a ruined castle, with gaping roof,*' she read. '*No doors, no windows just centuries of dust on the grey, stone floors. What happens when the wind blows up? A gentle breeze will stir the dust like a teaspoon in a sugar bowl. A howling gale will throw it in the air and spin it round. Either way, once the wind dies down, the picture's changed for ever. In some places, the dust will end up piled high, in others the layer will be thin, while in yet other parts you wouldn't know it was ever there.*'

She paused to cross her legs. The white go-go boots had been polished spotless. How on earth did these two manage it, Ruth wondered, picking yet another piece of burnt straw out of her hair.

'*So it is with rumour,*' the reporter chick continued. '*Particularly when you compare ruined castles to fishing villages that had been isolated until caravan holidays were all the rage, and trunk roads put them in reach of families for summer. There was nothing in Lisscombe to stop the rumours from swirling, and naturally some grow out of all proportion, some shrivel, and some of course will die. But by the time the dust dies down, the truth is changed.*'

She paused for effect.

'*Changed out of all recognition.*'

Suzanne lit a cigarette in flagrant disregard of the no-smoking sticker on the window, and curled her feet underneath her in a fluid feline gesture.

'That's very good. I like the rhythm of the writing.'

She blew a perfect smoke ring, and, as Ruth stacked her little blue and white vanity case in the rack above her seat, she wondered, was there ever a time this woman wasn't putting on an act for the public?

'Would you mind reading the piece about Lorelei, now?'

'My pleasure.'

Up on the cliff top, with everyone shielding their eyes, their noses, their mouths from the smoke, Ruth had assumed the journo was with the local rag.

Obviously not, if she was sitting next to Suzanne as the train pulled out of Lisscombe station. A London paper, then.

'You'd think a child born in the 40's and given the name Lorelei would be bullied, or at the very least teased, right the way through school. Not so. Among the predictable batch of Marys, Patricias, Sandras and Margarets ran a streak of envy at this rare, exotic name that came with mysterious, if not dangerous, overtones. Coupled, it has to be said, with relief that they hadn't been saddled with it themselves. And the boys? Oh, the boys were bewitched! From day one, they were enchanted by her delicate blonde beauty, quiet intelligence, and a temperament that was gentle but by no means a pushover. So you'd be forgiven for thinking that a child who was universally liked, got on with everyone, and fitted in everywhere would be spoilt for choice when it came to friends, but again, not the case. Lone wolf was the phrase used by her teachers. Self-contained was the term used by her mother.'

'Perfect! Absolutely perfect! Such a shame the gossips will never know I did them all a favour, keeping myself to myself after my husband and I bought that cottage.'

'They thought you'd inherited it. That the man who died was—' the reporter consulted her shorthand '—your uncle.'

'Think, think, think. That's all they've *ever* done. Oh, but just "think" what a let-down it would have been for them, poor souls, discovering Suzanne Cinq-Mars was overjoyed at finding herself pregnant. Far better to let them fabricate tales about backstreet abortions and booze—by the way, I don't drink, never have, you should write that down—and as for the trumpet player, well yes, I admit, he was a married man. Married to me. Jacques Cinq-Mars, you can write that down, too, born in Montreal.'

By this time, the train was joining the main line to London, and Ruth was laughing so hard, she was crying.

'You're going to hell, you know that?' she said.

'For putting on the best show Lisscombe's ever seen?' Suzanne threw up her hands. 'Darling, if that town had a pier, I'd have been the star at the end of it.'

The gossips lapped up every second of the past twenty-five years, she declared, and she was right. For an isolated fishing village, without television, cars, or even summer visitors to cater for in those empty, post-War days, entertainment was thin to say the least, and there were only so many radios you could listen to, card games to play, or Monopoly boards to roll out. Which left rumour-mongering. A skill in which certain ladies of the communities showed remarkable competence.

'Outrageous comments plus sweeping statements equals the perfect opportunity for Mrs. Busybody from the baker's and Mrs. Nosey Parker in the chemist's to put two and two together and make forty.'

Because, however loud Suzanne ramped up the volume, the music from her record player couldn't penetrate two feet of stone, any more than the squeals of tickle-fests could breach the defences of tightly packed reeds. Heck, not even bossy Mrs. Osborne rhymes-with-witch could see through the closed curtains behind which she read childrens' books out loud, made up stories, made up faces, clapping while Lorelei schlepped up and down in her mother's peach satin evening gown and high heeled shoes, tossing a feather boa over her shoulder the way Suzanne had taught her.

'As for Lorelei's father touring the world, so much better, don't you think, to let those silly women speculate about him abandoning me and disowning his child? While the knife is in my back, it's spared from someone else's. I just wonder where they imagined the money came from to pay the bills? Oh, and coastal erosion.'

She leaned over and tapped the reporter's pad with an immaculately varnished nail. Rapture pink, unless Ruth missed her guess.

'Make a note of that, please, it's important. That's the phrase that insurance johnny used when he came to assess the crack in the floor and down the wall. *Coastal erosion, rendering the building too dangerous for habitation.*'

'Most people would walk away,' Ruth murmured.

Suzanne wasn't most people. 'Darling, if they're going to demolish it, I might as well do the job for them.' She blew another smoke ring. 'Go out with a bang and all that.'

She'd hit that target right enough. God knows how long before the sound of timbers crashing in would fade from local minds, and no matter how much coffee Ruth swigged down, the taste of smoke remained bitter on her tongue. Jeez, it would be midnight, if she was lucky, before she could wash the stench and debris from her hair. This blouse was for the dustbin, that's for sure.

'Will you miss it?' she asked.

'Seagulls scavenging fish and chip wrappers tossed away by careless trippers, then splattering their thank-you's all over the place?' Suzanne's laugh was rich, cultured and, like that peach satin evening dress in the Paradise Club, infintely seductive. 'What do you think?'

'Actually,' Ruth said, 'I rather think you will.'

She might be going off to join her trumpet-playing husband, who earned more bread than ever on the cruise liners, but walking away from memories isn't easy. Memories like five-year-old Lorelei, squealing with delight as she buried her face in her mother's mink coat. Like poring over photographs together, while Suzanne told her daughter all about the maternal grandparents who died in the Blitz, but not before they'd held Lorelei in their arms—just once, but once was enough—because oh my, how they loved her!

'Exactly how much did you pay the fireman to bring that dressmaker's dummy out over his shoulder?' Ruth wondered.

Suzanne tipped her head back, showing perfect white teeth when she laughed. 'Let's say neither the police nor the fire benevolent funds did badly out of the arrangement.'

If you're going to do something, do it properly, was her motto. *No half measures.*

'This young lady, by the way, is writing an article for *Swing Music Magazine.* One of those where-are-they-now things.'

'When I started, I was pretty sure it would be jail.' That was the first time Ruth had seen the reporter smile. 'Then it twigged. Suzanne Cinq-Mars. War-time pin-up and singing sensation. Naturally, she staged the whole thing.'

'You were a pin-up?'

'Not a Forces Sweetheart like Vera Lynn, but yes. More than one fly boy tucked my photo under his pillow. Oh, I'm sorry.' She turned to the journo. 'This is my daughter. Goes by some silly name these days. Something about wanting to make it as a singer on her own.'

'Your mother's told me so much about you.' The reporter chick reached out to shake the hand Ruth twisted when she fell off her bike, breaking her ulna and collar bone in the process. 'Lorelei's a great name for a pop singer, y'know.'

Tell me about it, Ruth thought. Elvis? Cilla? Cher? Lorelei would have been fab—had pop been her bag.

And while the pencil scribbled down Suzanne's account of how her daughter left for a special school to train her voice for opera at fourteen, Ruth closed her eyes. Blocking out the clatter of wheels rattling over the track, Lorelei listened to her mother's voice ringing, pitch-perfect, across the flagstoned floor of a cottage that rang with laughter dawn to dusk.

'Pardon me, boy, is that the Chattanooga choo choo...'

Before another little echo chimed in.

'... track twenty-nine, can you give me a shine...'

NIGHT CROSSING

Mist rose like smoke over the river, emphasizing the cold and muffling sound. The only light in the cave came from a sconce set high on the wall, casting grotesque shadows as it gave off its distinctive odour of sulphur and lime. In all his years of helping people escape, he'd never once seen anyone replace that smooth, slender torch, but they must have. No rag on a stick burns that long. He waited.

It would not be long now.

Like the cold and the stench, waiting was something else he'd grown used to.

He shifted position. Beyond the cave, it was a different world. Out there, the night was warm. Sticky, even. Bats were on the wing in search of moths, boar snaffled freshly fallen acorns, owls swooped in the light of the moon. Creatures of the night every one, but they would not be alone. Apate, daughter of Night and Goddess of Deception, was bent over her loom, industriously weaving her mischief. At her shoulder stood Eris, her sister, mixing her famous brew of rivalry, discord and envy, until it fermented into misery thick enough to pour into a man's heart.

Zeus knows, that was a simple enough task at the best of times, but her job was ten times easier, now the autumn equinox had put paid to the campaigning season, the seas were closed to all but small fishing vessels, and the last of the harvests were in. Grape, grain, fruit and olive—

He tensed. Was that footsteps in the tunnel? Uh-uh. Just the slap-slap-slap of the water. Far in the distance a dog barked three times. Or maybe three dogs, barking once.

Reaching into the boat, he drew out a goat skin of wine and wondered why peace caused more trouble than war. Why men going off to fight far, far from home should make wives less faithful, not more, knowing their husbands were homesick and lonely, that they might well come back with serious injuries—assuming they came home at all. Or why resentment should rear its head when the harvest was brought in, as though it mattered who had the greater yield. Was that Eris's doing? Whispering how this person here was too lazy to nurture their crops? Or that person there sabotaged his neighbour's fields in the night?

As he drank, he mused how festivals only made matters worse. Yes, festivals, can you believe it? Processions, feasts, rituals, prayers. Times when everyone was supposed to rejoice, unwind, give thanks, take a breath before getting stuck in to ploughing, sowing, pressing the grapes or preparing for winter, but no.

Why's Gelon heading both the daytime and torchlight processions to honour Apollo? That's two years running he's done that.

Have you seen Melissa's new diadem? That didn't come from her husband.

How come the priests let Myron join the choir, not me? He sings like a donkey trapped in a thorn bush.

Such back-biting and bickering, you wouldn't believe. Throw in free wine and, whatever the celebration, it always ended up with women trading insults, men throwing punches and grudges growing bigger by the day.

Occasionally, though, darker obsessions come into play.

Obsessions colder than the water in this subterranean river...

This time the footsteps were real. Echoing with ghostly distortion along the tunnel of rock, like whispers passing through the House of Rumour.

'Sorry to keep you waiting.'

'You're paying me. That's all I care about.'

The coins chinked as they changed hands. He could tell from the weight it was what they'd agreed.

'This isn't fair!' Unlike her companion, whose voice was low, gruff, the voice of a man who wished he could be somewhere—anywhere—else, the woman's tone was sharp with indignation. 'I shouldn't be sneaking away like a thief in the night.'

'You killed her, Chloris, what did you expect? Life would carry on as before? Get in the boat.'

'No.'

'Please, Chloris.' Her companion cleared his throat. 'Don't make this harder than it already is.'

'She deserved it. You know it.'

'I know bad things will happen, if you stay. Listen.' In the distance, a horn blew, long, slow and mournful. 'You have to leave.'

'I could hide out here. Unless you knew where to look, who'd ever find this godforsaken cavern? Not with that scrambling fig over the entrance. Once the fuss has died down—'

'Now, Chloris.'

The boat rocked as her companion shoved her in, but strong hands on the oars kept it steady. The same strong hands that steered effortlessly through the mist swirling on the water. Closer now, the dog barked again. Same three barks.

'Because of *her*—'

When she clutched at his tunic, he could smell her perfume. Cinnamon, sweet rush and rose.

'—some cheap whore from the slums, he was going to divorce me. Send me back to my father, can you imagine the shame?' She started to cry. 'Eight years I put up with his drinking and philandering, washing his sweaty tunics, listening to him snore. *Oh, the poor wheelwright's wife,* that's how people saw me. Eight years never complaining, no voice of my own—then suddenly *she* comes along and the next thing, he's throwing me out and that bitch is raising my kids. You understand why she had to die, don't you?'

'I'm paid to transport you, not judge you.'

'Maybe so, but my actions were justified. Which is more than I can say for being forced out, so I'm begging you, please, in the name of all the gods on Olympus, turn back.'

'I can't.'

'Because of this?' She rattled the bag of coins. 'Is that all you care about, money?'

'Not entirely.' The side of the boat nudged the far bank. He threw the rope round a pole to secure it. 'But once you've crossed the Styx, there's no going back.'

Behind them, Cerberus' three heads each barked once.

Mist swirled like smoke over the water.

PIRATE OF PENANCE

He can't take his eyes off the spiral metal staircase leading down from the street. The sign on the door at the bottom reads *Heaven's Gate*. No one cares. They only see the flashing neon sign: *NUDES*. He can hear the heavy beat of music through the thick gray metal door. He senses the excitement and looks around. Men in bowler hats and pinstriped suits, carrying briefcases just like his. Men in trilby hats and raincoats. Women in miniskirts and bright red lipstick, with prices chalked on the soles of their shoes. His heart kicks, his mouth is dry. He knows he shouldn't. Descends anyway.

• • • •

SHE GIVES THE DISTINCTIVE knock-pause-knock-knock at the back, between the dustbins and the rats. *You're late.* Did he think she didn't know? Bleedin' bus didn't turn up, did it, which meant the second bus was packed. She ended up squashed among the smokers upstairs, and now she reeks of Player's Weights and Woodbines. *You're on in 10 minutes.* For Gawd's sake, she knows that, too! Gripping her fake snakeskin vanity case, she scurries to the dressing room. Halfway through changing, a bulb flickers twice, then dies. No matter, she can manage with just the one. On goes the eyeliner, the rouge, the false eyelashes thick as spiders. Three minutes later, there's her cue.

• • • •

HE'S ENGULFED BY A whirlpool of cigars, smoke and sex. Girls bump and grind to the hypnotic beat. They kick. They writhe. They flash a bit of leg, a bit of breast, was that a nipple? Too fast, they cover up. But with every sway and shake, every bend and twist and wiggle, their treasures are revealed. Ten-shilling notes litter the stage that's not a stage, just a cheap laminated board that runs the length of this seedy little club, where the lights are low and wooden seats (no tables) are spaced inches apart. The men come in alone, drinking but not drunk, bound by an invisible locker-room spirit. Behavior that would appall them all as individuals becomes acceptable in this anonymous dark crowd. He looks at the sinuous objects of their leering, clapping and whistling. The girls' fixed smiles. Dead eyes. *There's got to be a better life for them*, he thinks.

51

. . . .

INCH BY INCH, HER CLOTHES peel off, teasing all the way. Stockings always get the loudest whistle, coz they're usually the first to drop. She's not like the other girls. She keeps hers on. Even when there's nothing left and she's showing everybody Heaven's Gate, she keeps them on. Black fishnets, boy, that don't half get their juices goin'. Beyond the spotlight, she can see the surreptitious rubbing underneath their coats. No ten-bob notes for her. Uh-uh. They throw pound notes on the stage when she's performing. A whole quid, eh? Who'd have thought it? Just for a stupid pair of stockings. Her over-the-shoulder come-to-bed smile never falters as she wonders if she'll still be able to catch the last bus home and whether she can make the chip shop before it shuts. *There's got to be a better life*, she thinks.

. . . .

ALL NEXT DAY, HE SITS at his desk. Dullsville. Forms, reports, phone calls, faxes, meetings, poring over actuarial tables till his neck aches. No air. No windows. Just harsh fluorescent lighting and lunch in the canteen, where every day's predictable. Today, being Tuesday, it's sausage, mash and peas. His secretary is unmarried, fat and forty. Wouldn't know a smile from a fiver. His boss is plodding to retirement, not interested in anything except counting off the days and not rocking any boats. Stifled, bored, he knows he will be descending the forbidden spiral staircase after work.

. . . .

SHE SEES HIM, SAME seat three nights running, and her heart skips a beat. Could this be it? When she comes on stage, he leans forward, focusing on her and her alone. It could be, y'know. It could just be her ticket out of here. She shoots a smile straight at him. Directs her striptease at him. Makes bleedin' sure he knows this performance is for him, and him alone.

He can't believe it. She's so beautiful. So young. Tumbling dark curls. Tempting dark eyes. And she's looking at him. Not through him. *At* him. Giving herself to him, and him alone.

She has him. She bloody has. He's hooked. She gives him extra special attention with her routine the next night. Whispers: *If you're interested, I'm off at midnight.*

He waits. Sweating. Midnight—midnight!—and he's escorting a drop-dead-gorgeous girl to dinner! Nothing like this has ever happened in his plodding, predictable life. "Tell me about yourself," she says while the waiter pours wine.

Is she mad? Actuaries have the knack of making accountants look exciting. He's done nothing. Been nowhere. But Jesus bloody Christ.

She's passing her little pink tongue over her little pink lips. Think, man, think. Say something. Do something. "I'm not a poet, not a pirate, just a pawn," he says with a lopsided smile, then does the single most stupid thing he's ever done in his life. He magics a pound note out of her ear, shapes it into an *S*, attaches two paperclips—the joy of clerkdom, you always carry spare ones in your pocket—jerks the note, and while the clips spring off and miraculously join together, he pulls that silly trick where you fold your hands over each other, twist and turn, turn and twist, and make it look like your arms are made of rubber.

She laughs. The laugh is genuine. This isn't what she expected. No pawing. No groping. No dirty language, no springing of the age-old question: *How much?* He's the perfect gentleman. OK, not Rock Hudson or Paul Newman or Elvis or Cliff. But she's not Jean Shrimpton, either. He tells jokes, does magic tricks. Corny, but the way he tells them makes her giggle. To her surprise, she looks forward to their next date.

• • • •

THREE WEEKS LATER, and he's been down the staircase every weeknight after work, once even trekking into town on a Saturday, when he should have been—who cares where? What matters is: he was here. With her. He watches the girls gyrate to the music, teasing off their costumes inch by precious inch. Of course he watches the other girls. But it seems to him the leers are cruder now when the girl with the fishnets comes on, the jeers are louder, the gestures more coarse. So far, he's only ventured a couple of quick pecks, first on the cheek, next on the lips. His dreams, though, are far from chaste, and all of a sudden he is jealous of these filthy animals who have no connection or compassion for the girl with the dark, tumbling curls. They just want to ogle her breasts and glimpse Heaven's Gate, all the while making vulgar gestures with their tongues. If they had the chance, the bastards would take her like she was meat. His face is set, but deep inside, he boils with rage.

• • • •

SHE LOVES THE WAY HE performs card tricks on the restaurant table between courses. Especially the one where he lays the kings face up, the queens on top, then the jacks and then the aces, matching all the suits, puts them together, gets her to cut the pack three times, then, when he deals, out they come, all kings together, all four queens, four jacks, four aces. "I love you," he says, out of the blue. He feels silly, he adds nervously. It's so early in, but he does, he loves her, and he wants her to give up this seamy life. She spills her wine. Jesus. He isn't the Prince Charming she's dreamed of as a kid. His hair is starting to thin, he wears specs, he's the best part of twenty years older than her yet so bleedin' inexperienced, the only woman he talks about is his mother. But y'know what? He makes her laugh. He makes her laugh with his jokes and magic tricks and his impressions of everyone from Winston Churchill to Clint Eastwood to Laurel and Hardy. She invites him back to her bedsit on the Edgware Road. Gives herself to him.

• • • •

HE IS WALKING ON AIR. This lovely, lithe creature has opened her heart and her legs to him. He walks on air through phone calls and meetings, actuarial tables and reports. He catches himself whistling. Singing to himself. *He is in love.* For the first time in his pathetic, humdrum life, he is in love.

• • • •

AND SO IS SHE. HOLLYWOOD couldn't make this story up. The showgirl and the insurance clerk! Her young, him not so, her from the East End, him from Mill Hill, her lissome, him deskbound and pale. Oh, but what he makes her feel, though, in bed and out, is out of sight, babe. No one's ever put her on a pedestal before. No one's ever touched her the way he does, either, with tenderness and care. She's only eighteen, but, man, she's been putting it out for five years, has long since lost count of the number of men she's had and tears she's cried. Spellbound, she listens to the future he draws. "Two up and two down, nothing special," he says. "Two little girls, what shall we name them?" He'll build a rose bower in the garden, with a swing for the girls. She'll have his meal on the table when he comes home at night, she says—but only after he's taken her on it first! Oh, yeah. She'll be a good wife. The best wife *ever*. She'll cook and clean and scrub and polish. She'll have the sort of life she's always dreamed of. None of the raised voices, raised fists of her mother, or the uncles who used to come to her at night. He has saved her, and so what if the knight hasn't come galloping in on a white steed? Who wants drama when you can have magic tricks and silly jokes? So help her, she will love him with all of her heart for the rest of her life and beyond.

• • • •

HE DOESN'T UNDERSTAND. There's no pain, yet at the same time he can't move. His limbs won't move, his hands won't work, his vision is hazy and white. There is panic. He can't breathe. What—what's happening...?

"You lied to me," she hisses. "You said you loved me. You told me I was the only woman for you."

You are, he wants to say, *oh, God, you are,* but his mouth won't let the words out. Through the haze, he sees something sharp and bright and shiny coming down. Again, again, again.

"Then this sour-faced bitch collars me outside the club," she says. Her hands, her face, her clothes are wet with blood, she doesn't notice. "Calls me a tart, a slut and that's just for starters. Tells me to leave her husband alone, and I laughed, can you believe it? I actually bloody laughed. Told her to sod the hell off, I'm no home wrecker, me."

I'm sorry, he wants to say, *I'm so very, very sorry,* but he can't speak because of some weird gargling sound. Where's that coming from? For one silly, stupid moment, he thinks it might be him.

"Then she shows me these photos," she says, showering him with the prints that she's snatched. "You, the wife, two kids. Girls. 'What shall we name them?'

At the beach at Margate. At the Tower of London. In your own bleedin' back garden. 'Two up, two down, nothing special.'"

The last thing he sees is a photograph. It's the rose bower that he built last summer. Funny, he could have sworn the flowers were white—but look, they're red.

'Sister Mary Joseph?'

That was the first surprise. How, after all this time, his voice hadn't changed a note. Still deep. Cultured. Soft as brandy butter.

'When the boy told me a Bride of Christ, an English one no less, wanted to meet me on Boot Hill, I feared it was a leg-pull.'

I dragged my eyes away from the rooftops of Tombstone, shimmering in the desert sun half a mile below. Rooftops which, until eight years ago, housed more than twenty times the current population. And witnessed far too many killings.

'Not a prank, I assure you, Mr. Bradbury.' I turned. 'Thank you trailing all the way up here on such a fiendishly hot afternoon.'

He chuckled. 'Obviously you are new to the Arizona Territory, Sister, or you'd know that all our afternoons are fiendishly hot.'

I let my breath out. Very, very, very, very slowly. He didn't recognize me, but why would he? Eleven years had passed since our paths last crossed, and let's face it. How many men look twice at middle-aged nuns?

I forced a smile. 'Two days is not *quite* enough to become familiar with the climate.'

Much less adapt.

'No doubt you find our terrain somewhat alien, as well. All this prickly pear and sagebrush. Not quite the majestic oaks and beech woods you're used to, is it?'

'Personally, I am more concerned with your majestic scorpions and rattlesnakes.'

'Surely,' he laughed, 'they are all God's creatures?'

'Which, I am convinced, He placed in this inhospitable corner of the universe expressly to remain undisturbed.'

His laugh deepened. 'Spring cannot be the easiest of seasons to cross the Atlantic. Was it rough?'

I focused on a butterfly taking nectar from the yellow flower of a cactus. Listened to a wren trilling from the top of a rickety post. Pretended the black creatures circling in the sky to the north were not vultures.

Dear Reverend Mother,

I hope this letter finds you and the Sisters well, that the chapel roof has now been patched, and Sister Mary Francis is recovered from her fall.

So many terrible things have befallen us since you waved us off at the dockside that I scarcely know where to begin. And even there, the crossing was nothing like we had been led to believe.

Apart from being hopelessly overcrowded with horrendously inadequate washrooms, there were no hooks on which to hang clothes, no bins, no privacy, and although the dormitory floors were swept daily, they were not scrubbed. Consequently, vomit dried where it spewed, and it was hardly surprising that many passengers, myself included, spent most of the voyage on deck, where we were much hampered by the pitch and toss of the ship, as well as the most unimaginable clutter of machinery and equipment you have ever seen in your life, while constantly showered with hot cinders from the smoke stack.

All of which one could bear with fortitude, had it not been for the death of Kenan Trevarrow.

Until the copper ran out, Cornwall had been the most heavily industrialized region in the world. Many mine owners subsequently turned to their hands to tin, and successful they were, too. Tin might be deep and dangerous to extract, but being a key component in brass, it was in constant demand, and as such commanded a high price. All the same, tin production wasn't remotely on the scale of copper and, like it or not, the glory days were over. Mines closed. Men found themselves without work. Merchants had nothing to trade. Then news trickled in about gold and silver mines in Australia and the Americas, sparking a mass migration of skills. Not merely miners, refiners, smelters and foundry men, but farmers and powder men, tradesmen and engineers, all eager to make their fortune elsewhere.

Mr. Trevarrow was a pit man. Typical of the breed, being tall, broad and strong. But six days into the crossing his heart gave out, and the poor fellow died on the deck where he fell. To this day, Reverend Mother, Mrs. Trevarrow's howls still haunt my dreams. Her agony, I should add, was not at being left with three children and no means of support. Widowhood was a spectre she had lived with her whole life, the mines being such perilous places. As you know only too well, every month there'd be falls from the exhausting ladder climbs from shafts a thousand feet below. Of men dying horribly from lung rot. Fatalities from underground explosions caused by fumes or badly laid dynamite. Happily (if that's the word), I was able to persuade Mrs. Trevarrow to join the little group you had entrusted to my care.

Her torment, I'm afraid, came from learning that her husband would not be buried in sacred ground. I never imagined such wickedness existed! To be denied the chance to rise on the Day of Judgment beggars belief, but despite our pleas, the captain refused to budge on the matter. Kenan Trevarrow was tossed overboard, without not so much as a pinch of blessed soil inside the rough canvas that was his shroud.

This, Reverend Mother, was the first of many heartbreaks we encountered—'

'Rough?' I composed my face. 'Dear me, no, Mr. Bradbury. My transatlantic cruise was most restful, thank you.'

'Then things have changed since my day. We used to call them coffin ships, conditions on board were so dire.'

My day? He was scarcely older than me. Certainly not yet fifty. But then one forgets how young the men were, how terribly young, when they came West, seeking their fortunes.

'I must confess, it's a rare treat, conversing with another English person,' he was saying. 'For all that it is virtually a ghost town now, Tombstone remains a babble of German, Russian, Irish, Chinese—' He paused. 'Apache. But I'm rambling. I apologize. What exactly can I do for you, Sister?'

Perspiration drenched the inside of my habit. Pooled on my skull beneath the wimple.

'For one thing, Mr. Bradbury, you could remove that Peacemaker from your waistband. This being the Lord's ground.'

'Of course.' His smile was tight. Confused. Did he think I hadn't noticed the ivory handle poking out? Or that nuns don't recognize a hand gun when they see one? 'Forgive me.'

He laid the Colt on a pile of rocks marking a grave whose rough hewn cross read *Rook. Shot by a Chinaman.* I presumed Rook was a man, rather than a bird, and idly wondered whether his assassin had any connection with the young man chip-chip-chipping out a grave in the Chinese corner of the cemetery.

'Along with the little cap lock pistol in your boot, please.'

'Ah. Sorry. I'd forgotten about that.'

He hadn't.

But more importantly, neither had I.

'Do you mind if we move to the shade?' I made the sign of the cross over the weapons and sighed. 'Such as it is.'

Dust from the gravel left a grey line round my hem as I picked my way up the hill to a scrubby specimen close to where the young Chinaman was digging. Along the way, I took care to keep my eyes on the mountains, hazy and purple in the distance, and not the piles of rocks that covered the dead. Their wonky wooden markers. Epitaphs that talked of violence and retribution, rather than peaceful ends in old age. But this, of course, was how this cemetery got its name.

After men who'd died with their boots on.

—the first of many heartbreaks we encountered—

'I'm hoping you can help me, Mr. Bradbury. I am looking for someone.'

'With all due respect, Sister, I can't imagine why you think I'm the man for the job.'

'You own a gambling saloon, do you not? *The Ace in the Hole?*'

Not that you'd suspect it from his appearance. Admittedly, his clothes reflected the recent downturn in prosperity, being a year or two behind the times, and not a little threadbare at the elbows and knees. But his boots were polished, his collar clean, and his black felt derby recently brushed. Indeed, in his cotton sack coat, Comstock vest and red silk bow tie, James Bradbury could pass for a hotelier, a bank clerk, or a patent medicine salesman.

The latter not entirely inappropriate.

Snake oil being his stock in trade.

'That I do, Sister.'

'With a sign outside that reads *Whisky—Gambling—Dancing Girls?*'

'Without wishing to be pedantic, the sign reads <u>Very</u> Good *Whisky—Gambling—Dancing Girls*. None of that rotgut coffin varnish brewed from raw spirit and burnt sugar, with a splash of chewing tobacco for us. Uh-uh. I have only ever served the finest quality bourbon and rye, not forgetting, of course, champagne for special occasions, or that other mainstay of ours, beer. Always with clean towels hanging from the bar, so the *Ace's* patrons can wipe the froth from their beards.'

'You make it sound almost respectable, Mr. Bradbury.'

'If you're here to save my immortal soul, you're thirty years too late. And without wishing to labour the point, just because I own a saloon, it doesn't follow that I know everybody in town.'

His immortal soul didn't concern me.

'But you do know everyone in your end of town?'

'Now why on earth would you think that?'

Why? Because in the two days since I arrived, I'd familiarized myself with every inch of these abandoned, boarded up streets. I wanted—needed—to understand what the place was like during the boomtown years, when it churned out an eye-popping $40,000,000 in silver bullion alone.

How it dealt with the death blow after a well was drilled to provide the growing population with water, and what started out as seepage quickly flooded the mines to the point that no amount of pumping could stop it.

But especially what it was like for the people who made Tombstone their home.

All too often in the literal sense.

—the first of many heartbreaks we encountered—

'Correct me if I'm wrong, Mr. Bradbury, but isn't Allen Street the dividing line between the residential area to the north, with its banks, churches, even a fine opera house, and the...' I chose my words carefully, timed the pause better '...leisure quarter? Where I'm told—' (Lord forgive me, I counted) '—over a hundred honkytonks, gambling halls, opium dens and bordellos plied their trade until recently? And that the *Ace in the Hole* is one of the few saloons still to be trading?'

He ran his finger round the inside of his collar. There wasn't room enough for two under this tree.

'For a new girl in town, you seem to know an awful lot about the place.'

I had no intention of explaining that until I alighted from the stage coach—the railroad never did make it this far—all I'd known about this bleak frontier town was what most people knew.

That Wyatt Earp once marshalled this most lawless of settlements. That and his brothers ran with Doc Holliday, inveterate gambler, dentist, gunslinger and consumptive, who died what? must be five or six years ago now. And it was home to the *OK Corral*, site of the most famous gunfight in history. Of which, incidentally, only the sign remains to bear witness, after a fire ripped through the district so fast, and causing so much destruction, that the only way to stop it had been to dynamite the buildings in its path.

But I'd put my two days to exceptional use. I'd asked questions, a lot of questions, and learned fast.

I needed to.

—the first of many heartbreaks we encountered—

'I know why many people might want to call themselves by different names when they came West,' I said smoothly.

The veneer slipped only a little. 'If you're suggesting I'm using an alias—'

'I'm suggesting no such thing, Mr. Bradbury.'

I knew fine well he was.

'I'm merely pointing out that—well. New identity, new start? Makes perfect sense.'

The young Chinaman continued to excavate with rhythmic precision, as though a nun and gambler standing ten feet away was a normal and everyday occurrence. And dear me, if any place on God's earth reflected the accuracy of dust to dust, it was surely this barren land. While I planned my words, I watched him work, that ultimate symbol of Chinese manhood and dignity—the braided pigtail—swinging black and shiny beneath his coolie hat. Something else I'd picked up on my travels. That Chinese for hard labour was *ku li*.

'I was thinking more along the lines that nicknames are not exactly uncommon in these parts,' I said. 'Black Bart, Billy the Kid, Texas Jack—'

'Russian Bill.' Bradbury's face creased with something close to affection. 'Now *there* was a man of culture, Sister. Curly blond hair, snappy dresser, spoke four languages, did our Bill, including Russian, although no one ever believed his tale about being a Russian aristocrat. But my, that fellow would pin you to the ground, talking science, art or literature with anyone who'd listen. Which was not many, I might add, but God rest his hanged soul, he was not your average cattle rustler, that's for sure.'

Quite the ladies' man, too, from what I could gather. Rented a box in the Birdcage Theater for $25 a night, when the average daily wage was $4, entertaining showgirls behind the thick velvet curtains. Like many establishments, the theater had been boarded up these past three years, but I'd managed to push past one of the panels.

The dancers and banditos were long gone, of course, but close your eyes, breathe deeply, and you could still feel the notoriety. In the bullet holes that riddled the walls. (Sixteen gunfights no less). In the rosewood piano, decaying softly in the stillness. The vibrant lithographs on the walls, of acrobats, trapeze artists and bareback riders painted by a Swede who'd never set foot in a circus. Nothing inside the Birdcage had changed. The mahogany bar might have been waiting for the doors to swing open for business. The curtains on the stage looked set to part any second. And was it that table in the corner, beneath the stairs, that witnessed the longest poker game in history? Eight years, five months, three days, I was told. With Doc Holliday one of its many players.

'I'm beginning to understand why you need my help,' Bradbury said.

The searing heat had reddened his face. He mopped his brow with a yellow silk handkerchief, and I wondered how people could survive in such treacherous heat, weighed down by frock coats and vests. Much less why they would want to.

'The man you're trying to track down calls himself by another name now, and you're hoping that, by describing him, I'll be able to point him out?'

Not exactly.

'Well, with all due respect, Sister, even if he was my best bar-keep, if a fellow doesn't want to be found, far be it for me to sell him out.'

Something scuttled round the base of an agave. Please, *please* let it be a lizard of one kind or another. I'd heard there were spiders in this desert big enough to cover a man's hand, and that lived on a diet of mice. The last thing I needed was to be terrified into losing my resolve.

Or shocked into making a mistake.

'Calamity Jane, Belle Starr, Stagecoach Mary,' I said calmly. 'Who worked in a Mission, did you know that?' Up in Montana, if memory served. 'Leastways, until the bishop kicked her out. Something to do with whisky, swearing and a six-shooter, I believe. My point being, it's not only men and outlaws who acquire nicknames out West.'

'I'd hate you think I was being obstructive here, Sister, but the ladies who go by different names in these parts—the likes of Butter Brown, Big Nose Kate, Madame Mustache—tend to be what we refer to as "soiled doves". They work out of the bordellos—'

'China Mary isn't a prostitute.'

For a moment, I thought there was a break in the grave digger's rhythm. My mistake. Chip-chip-chip, the pit grew ever longer and deeper, reminding me of the Chinese custom to inter the bodies for exactly one year, after which they would be dug up, cleaned, and the bones soaked in brandy to preserve them. They would then be wrapped in the finest silk, placed in an urn and shipped home to the Pearl Delta, where they would be re-buried with full mourning rites, sacrificial objects and rituals, and worshipped at the family shrine.

'China Mary's a different kettle of fish altogether.'

'Any woman who controls the whole of Hoptown has to be,' I said.

Bradbury looked at me with a mixture of surprise (that I knew so much about this town), and irritation (that I wouldn't let go). But in New York, San Francisco, indeed every city I know, such migrant quarters are called Chinatown. In Tombstone here, the oriental population was so extensive that it occupied the areas from 1st to 3rd Street, as well as Freemont to Toughnut, and was dubbed Hoptown, because the inhabitants "hopped" between them via connecting tunnels.

And China Mary had a grip on it all.

Immaculately kitted out in jade, brocaded silks and sporting the largest earrings this side of the moon, you wouldn't think, to look at her enviably smooth complexion and feminine fan, that she ran everything from laundries to restaurants, gambling halls to opium dens, laundries to stores with a grip harder than a Wyoming winter.

For most people, *tongs* conjure up images of gangsters and thugs. Far from it. Like the Irish, the coastal crofters of Scotland, and the Highlanders displaced in the infamous Clearances, the poverty-stricken inhabitants of the Pearl Delta were forced to look beyond their homeland to survive. The *tongs* found them work—in this case, on *Gum Shan*, Golden Mountain—drew up detailed employment contracts, paid their passages, found them accommodation, and took care of them when they fell ill. Because the new territories were lawless and wild, the *tongs* set no faith in banks or the likes of Wells Fargo, acting as bankers and deliverymen—but woe betide any worker who stepped out of line.

While the mines were mostly worked by Germans, Cornishmen and the Irish, the Chinese labour force turned its hand to construction work, laundries and food. As the residential area expanded, so it became fashionable to employ them as houseboys and servants, but no worker could be hired without going through China Mary first. *They steal, I pay* was her motto. A policy that went hand in hand with never turning anyone away, Chinese or white, who was in need of help, earning her universal respect.

Well, almost.

'I don't hold with Chinks. Devious, cunning, corrupt little bast—blighters, the lot of them. Shovel food in their mouths with a couple of twigs, eat kittens in batter I'm told, and caterpillars in stew, and the ugly little buggers squat like hogs while they're doing it.' He shuddered. 'Unnatural. All that scented smoke and chanting. God knows what mischief they're plotting.' He tipped his hat. 'Pardon my blasphemy, Sister.'

Something scuttled above me in the scrubby mesquite.

I ignored it.

Concentrated on trying to breathe.

—*the first of many heartbreaks we encountered*—

'Neither your blasphemy nor your bigotry concern me, Mr. Bradbury.'

I stepped out from under the shade of the tree. Sweat had glued fabric to skin. My tongue was stuck to the roof of my mouth.

'I am simply trying to track down a young woman.'

I clasped my hands behind my back, so he would not see them shaking.

'Who lies here. On Boot Hill.'

. . . .

TO UNDERSTAND THE GRAVEYARD, I had to understand the town.

From when a lone prospector struck pay dirt in hills where he'd been warned that "the only thing you find up there is your tombstone".

How rich seams close to the surface turned a ragtag bunch of tents, shacks and cabins into a ridiculously prosperous settlement of fourteen thousand souls.

Who promptly turned on one another.

They fought over claims, they fought over property, they robbed banks that contained their own money. They rustled cattle and held up stage coaches, they swindled, raped, stole horses and more, nearly all at the point of a gun. Single men for the most part, tensions ran permanently high, and no wonder Boot Hill was full of epitaphs of men who had been hanged or else shot in a gunfight. Some even comically so. *Here Lies Lester Moore, Four Slugs from a .44. No Les. No More.* The three cattle thieves who fell at the *OK Corral* were here, buried side by side. Even poor Rook, killed by a Chinaman.

Some call it Gold Fever.

The rest of us call it greed.

Either way, many of these sorry mounds had no markers at all. Just lumps of rock covering unknown, unnamed individuals, who'd died before they could answer the most basic question of all.

Who are you?

And more importantly, who are your kin, so we can inform them?

. . . .

In the end, Kenan Trevarrow's widow did not join us on the wagon train west. Not born into farming stock, and intending to follow her husband to the mines, she could not envisage a life on the Plains. We left her in New York, hopeful of finding work with an Austrian baker.

Sadly, she was not the only one we left behind.

Do you remember the Dyer family, Reverend Mother? It would appear that the agent from whom they bought their claim was a fraudster.

The land belonged to somebody else, paid for fair and square—can you believe the scoundrel didn't even fulfil his bargain to pay their way on the train? Consequently, the poor souls lost every farthing through one man's greed and deceit, and tragically, they were far from alone. Many families, we discovered, had met the same fate, swindled of their savings and left high and dry. Indeed, the Fentons were only able to continue because they sold every stick of furniture in New York to pay their way.

HOW THEY EXPECTED TO buy grain and animals when they arrived, I had no idea, much less build a house. But if there's one thing I'd learned since leaving Plymouth, it was the resilience of the human spirit.

"For I know the thoughts that I think toward ye, sayeth the LORD, thoughts of peace and not of evil, to give ye a future and hope."

Jeremiah 29:11.

Week after week, our faith was tested by snow-capped mountains, endless prairies, swollen rivers and torrential storms. We battled dust, heat and flies, exhaustion, loneliness, and discomfort. Twice, we passed the graves of earlier pioneers who had been attacked by Indians, heard the blood chilling tales of the survivors, and on one memorable occasion, actually saw the charred remains of four wagons. All of which strengthened our resolve to remain in large groups at all times, for it was only the small parties that were picked off.

But in the end, we were not beaten by either the elements or by savages. We were beaten, Reverend Mother, by disease.

· · · ·

'PERHAPS IF YOU DESCRIBE the woman who's buried here, Sister, it might ring a bell.' Bradbury indicated the deserted sprawl in the distance. 'Though I should warn you. In the boom years, girls passed through Tombstone like water over the rapids.'

I felt myself swaying. Told myself not to pass out. Not here. Not now. Without knowing.

'Dark hair, blue eyes, skinny as a rake—' My heart thumped. '—sang like a linnet, she did. No?'

'Uhhhh....'

'She'd have been sixteen when she arrived, twenty-seven when she died. The priest baptized her Charlotte Jane.'

'Sorry, Sister.'

'She worked at the *Ace in the Hole*.'

'Ah! Champagne Charlie! Of course.' His smile was pure oil. 'Charming creature, astonishing voice as you quite rightly said. But if you're worried she was more dove than linnet...?' He wagged a playful finger. 'Dancing girls are just that, Sister. Paid to entertain the clientele while they recover from a hard day at the seam over a drink or two in the saloon, or sing while the miners indulge in a hand of faro.'

'I believe their role's a little broader than that, Mr. Bradbury. Especially at the *Ace in the Hole*.'

Men would part with a quarter of their daily salary for just one dance with the girls, who weren't paid by Bradbury, not at all. Their income was purely commission-based. Some from their minuscule percentage of the dance fee. Most from the drinks the men bought them, which were not only marked up at twice their wholesale price, but were invariably nothing more than cold tea served in a shot glass, naturally charged at full price. The prettier the saloon girl, the sweeter her voice and the harder she flirted, the more she could earn.

Up to $10 a week during the boom years.

When miners and mill workers pocketed $4 a day.

'Champagne Charlie?' Was that croak really me?

'Partly a pun on her name. Inspired by that English music hall fellow, you know who I mean? But mainly because to these uncouth cowboys and miners, she came over classy and cultured.'

'Making them more susceptible to buying expensive bottles of champagne?'

He buffed his neatly barbered whiskers. 'What can I say, Sister? A man has to make a dollar where he can.'

'I see.' I certainly did. 'And now we've established her identity, do you mind telling me exactly which of these unmarked graves is hers?'

'Ah. Well. You need to understand, times are hard. The old green cloth isn't as busy as it used to be, Sister. The men don't have spare cash to buy dancers—'

'Is that why you wouldn't allow her to leave?'

Charlotte was the *Ace's* star asset. The only reason it stayed open after the mines flooded. Her sweet voice and sweeter nature...

'She was better off here, Sister. I mean, where would she go? She was an orphan. And when she died, forgive me for not remembering the date, a year ago maybe—'

'Let's say two.'

'All right, two, but you have to understand. The only thing stopping Tombstone from turning into a ghost town was the Courthouse. We're still the centre of justice in Cochise County, thank God—'

Who could miss the twin nooses hanging from the gallows opposite, their ropes swaying gently, despite the lack of breeze? As though beckoned by the unseen hand of retribution.

'—but when the mines ran out, so did the money.'

'You couldn't run to fashioning her a rough wooden cross?'

'I, um—you know I'm sure we had one. Must have blown away. Dust storm. Something. I, er, I'll arrange to have one erected. Another one. Obviously. But, look, since you've travelled such a long way to find her, it's that one.'

He pointed to a small heap of rocks between *Unknown, Hanged by Mistake* and *Dutch Joe, Murdered, 1886.*

Despite the heat, and my resolve, I shivered.

'So then.' He rocked on his heels. 'Now you've found Charlie—Charlotte, what are your plans, Sister?'

I turned away from *Unknown* and *Dutch Joe.* Took a moment to follow the vultures, still circling high in the sky to the north. Squinted into the heat haze over the rooftops. Listened to the rhythmic chip-chip-chip of the shovel. Then I let out the breath I'd been holding and smiled. A genuine, fulfilled, cat got the cream smile, and suddenly my hands were no longer shaking, I no longer felt sick.

'Exactly what I set out to do when I left home, Mr. Bradbury.' My voice held no tremors, either. 'I'm sending you straight to hell.'

• • • •

FOR A MAN ACCUSTOMED to violence, he was pretty slow on the uptake. Three times, his mouth opened and closed like a goldfish, but there's nothing like a bullet bouncing off your thigh bone to concentrate the mind.

And that's the thing about the desert.

No one can hear you scream.

Ten feet away the young Chinaman stopped. He looked at Bradbury, howling, cursing, in a sea of blood. Looked at me. Looked back at Bradbury. Then calmly carried on digging.

'For pity's sake, Sister, have mercy! Whatever you think, I didn't kill her—'

'You beat her.'

'Once. I lost my temper. I'm sorry.'

'Repeatedly.'

'No, no, I swear—'

'Then one day, you took it too far. You threw her down the stairs.'

My second bullet went through the top of his chest. I heard his right shoulder blade shatter. Who would have thought a man could scream so loud?

'It was an accident! For the love of God, Sister, call a doctor.'

'The last doctor packed up and left three years ago.'

'Mule doctor. Barber. Anyone!' He appealed to the young man, chipping away. 'China Mary. Fetch China Mary! She'll help. Please. Please, I'm dying.'

Bradbury might have been invisible. There was no change to the rhythm.

Heading west through Missouri, tragedy struck. Later, the Wagon Master would claim the drinking hole had been poisoned by Indians, though I find the explanation unlikely. Why would they poison their own water supply? The priest, who buried Mrs. Hunter's baby, blamed contamination from a dead animal, probably a cow. The truth is, we shall never know the reason so many of us fell ill, and why eleven of our party died.

Charlotte's father was the first.

I cradled him in my arms to the end, but by now I had the fever myself, as had Charlotte. The train couldn't stop. Far too dangerous. But by the time we reached Springfield, many of us were too ill to continue, and

I thanked the Holy Father when we were befriended by a man called James Bradbury.

His support didn't come cheap, but I'll be honest. After the tragedies we had encountered along the route, I would have given my life savings, my own life, my soul to save Charlotte.

When he told me she was dead, I wanted to die. Prayed for release from the torment. But God spared me, Reverend Mother—

'You're not dying,' I told him. 'At least not yet.'

'You're a nun, you can't do this!'

'I'm not a nun, Mr. Bradbury.' I pulled off the sodden habit and wimple, exposing the floral cotton frock underneath. 'I'm a mother. Charlotte's mother, if you must know. In Springfield, Missouri, you told me she was dead. Even showed me her grave.'

For eleven years, I had been laying flowers beside a stranger's headstone.

'And you told her I was dead, too, in order to take her to Tombstone and put her to work.'

He stole her mother, her life, her future, her hope—for the sake for a few silver dollars.

The third bullet went straight between his eyes.

• • • •

'YOU NO NEED DO THIS,' the young Chinaman said. 'You go see daughter.'

'After eleven years, another hour won't matter, Chen.'

We had rolled him into the waiting grave, now we were piling boulders on top of the body.

'I killed him. It's only right that I help bury him.'

'Me tell you yesterday. I happy kill him.' The pigtail swung back and forth with the same rhythmic precision as when he'd been digging. 'Chinese workers pay him much dollar. He promise to ship urn to Pearl Delta. Many urn. He no do. He take dollar, take silk, throw bones in desert.'

Flaunting his trophies in the form of handkerchiefs and bow ties.

'Ancestors no have worship now. No have rest.'

I thought of the letter I'd written so, so long ago to my dear cousin who had taken Holy Orders, about Kenan Trevarrow, buried at sea—

—*the first of many heartbreaks we encountered*—

—and of the letter which eventually found me in Springfield, Missouri, where I had stayed after the death of my husband and only child. The letter signed by Mei Choy. A woman known throughout Tombstone as China Mary. The same woman who kept a tight grip on Hoptown, but who would never turn away anyone who needed help.

Including a dark-haired saloon girl enslaved to the *Ace in the Hole*, who'd crawled, broken and bloodied, to her for treatment before planning to run away in the night. But then James Bradbury found her, and hurled her down the stairs.

If he couldn't have her, nobody could.

It was a miracle Mei Choy's letter found me at all. Apparently, Charlotte had spoken of my cousin, the Reverend Mother, in Plymouth. By the time the letter reached her, then crossed the Atlantic again, only to travel another thousand miles with Wells Fargo, over eighteen months had gone by.

But as the desert sun beat down on Charlotte's grave, a yellow cactus blooming at the side of the mound, so my heart warmed, and I recalled another famous saying about Tombstone. That it ate a man for breakfast each morning.

Watching Chen cover Bradbury's body with boulders, I was pretty sure Boot Hill was pleased with its latest meal.

SCHOOL OF HARD ROCKS

It's a mammoth job, being a caveman. Take last month, when the wife wanted a new sofa. A whole a fortnight it took me to chip that bloody thing out of the rock, and what does she say? Why couldn't I have chiselled out a three-seater? As for fashion, don't get me started. One minute pelts with spots are all the rage, next it's stripes, and this year my daughters tell me they won't be seen *dead* wearing fur that isn't pastel.

'Bit ironic, don't you think?' I asked the eldest. 'Considering the fox they came from is long since deceased?'

Teenagers, eh? Didn't so much as look up from her tablet, just kept chipping away at the thing, but trust me, silence beats the customary want-something whine. I count the days, you have no idea, when some young buck drags her off by the hair, but that sneer of hers puts them right off. Between you and me, who can blame them?

'Exactly where do you think you're going, missy?'

The younger one turned in the cave mouth. 'Duh. It's Saturday.'

'So?'

'So I only go clubbing on Saturdays, don't I.'

'Better take this, then.' I tossed her my big club, the one studded with claws.

'Wow.' Her scowl popped like a bubble. 'Thanks, Dad!'

I'm Jim, by the way. Head of the Birch Tree tribe, and when I'm not at the mercy of a sulky wife and two hormonal daughters, I teach art at the School of Hard Rocks.

It's said *those who can do, those who can't teach*, but in practice life's not that simple. Ever since the tribes put their differences aside and voted to stylise our sacred paintings, artistic skills need to be honed. And to all those who tell you it's tough being a hunter or a gatherer, to them I say, try teaching pigments and proportion to a bunch of hopefuls who can't tell their aurochs from their ibex.

Few make the grade. The patience and discipline that is required puts most students off, because like it or not, the world's changing. The history books are growing fast. We have two slabs now, instead of just one, and a sad sign of the times is that the only thing kids want today is fast food (yeah, like that gazelle's going to stop in its tracks and wait to be speared) and a career in tech support,

73

but honestly. A constant barrage of smoke signals has to be bad for their health, just as hunched over a fire, day in day out, is going to leave them with appalling backache one day.

'You're such a dinosaur,' number one daughter bleats at every opportunity, but she's young. She doesn't understand. Someone has to keep the old ways alive, and if the holy men and cave painters don't leave art for posterity, how will future generations know we even existed?

But every so often a rare talent shines through. An artist, whose creativity transcends everything that went before. Bruce from the Spruce tribe is one such example. With breathtaking flair, he layers horse over bison, antelope over zebra, manes flaring every one, to create a stampede. Art like that? Makes the prickles rise on the back of your neck, because when you look at Bruce's work, I swear you can hear the thunder of hooves and find yourself coughing from his painted dust.

Abel from Maple Tree tribe is another. He took the concept of handprints on flat walls and took it to another dimension by blowing paint over every hand of very member of every tribe, leaving prints for eternity, all pointing west to the land of our ancestors, but in such a joyous wave pattern it looks like a crowd throwing their hands up for joy.

When I look at Bruce Spruce and Abel Maple, my heart swells.

'Between them, those boys are eroding tribal rivalry and bringing the nations together,' I told my wife. 'You can't believe how proud I am of my pupils.'

'Precisely why,' she said, narrowing her eyes in the way you know something bad is about to tumble out of her mouth, 'you need to find who killed Pranksy.'

'Very funny.' Not. 'That's Plod's job, and you know it.'

'Plod's a fine investigator, Jim, but Abel Maple's his cousin, and who knows how objective he'll be, when it comes to family.'

Birch tribe had a bent copper once. Or maybe a bent copper birch. I forget. The point is, 'You don't honestly think Abel killed Pranksy?'

'If you ever watched *Murder She Chiselled*, you'd know you can't rule anyone out as a suspect.'

'That's fiction, this is real life, and I'm only a teacher.'

'Who inspired Bruce Spruce and Abel Maple to achieve greatness, just as your mentoring inspired Pranksy to produce his own special art.'

'Don't flatter it, love. It's graffiti, pure and simple, and subversive graffiti at that.'

'We all make satirical political statements, Jim.'

'Not on walls we don't.'

Pranksy didn't paint his rebellious messages inside, either. Plastered every public surface he could find, and, worse, carried out his handiwork under cover of darkness.

'And if you're trying to make me feel responsible for the way he turned out, love, forget it. I've had tons of failures, not just Pranksy.'

But you know women. Once they set their mind to something, that's it. End of. *Just find Pranksy's killer, Jim, or it's the spare cave for a month.*

To my credit, I held out three whole nights.

• • • •

'WHY WOULD YOUR WIFE want *you* to find Pranksy's killer?'

Sitting with the medicine woman beside the river that ran through the gorge, watching eagles soar in a cloudless blue sky while the breeze whispered through the leaves and the scent of herbs drifted on the air, it was impossible to imagine murder stalking such beauty and peace.

'Why is the earth flat?' I shrugged. 'If I knew how women's minds worked, I'd still be single and happy.'

Kwin laughed. 'Liar. You wouldn't have it any other way.'

One thing I've learned from living in a harem : never tell a woman she's right.

'I hear you examined the body,' I said instead. 'Is that normal?'

'It is, when it's the first thing you see when you open your cave screen in the morning.'

'Come again?'

'Pranksy, bless him, was sprawled out, not a handspan from where you're standing now.'

I jumped back from the stain on the grass that, until then, hadn't warranted a second glance. Blood goes with the territory of being a medicine woman, while animals are routinely butchered for food. But when it's the life force of a young man you'd known all his life... Someone you taught and whose talent you nurtured...

'Pranksy was killed here?'

'Technically—' She broke off at the sound of a horn blowing, and picked up two smooth stones laid out on her tree stump. 'Scuse me a sec, that's my vasectomy patient.'

Two gasps and a strangled cry later, Gud from Fir tree tribe limped away, face pale, eyes watering like crazy. Poor sod would be Gud Fir nothing, I thought, wincing. But then I didn't have ten kids running round, needing to be fed. Who was I to judge?

'Sorry about that,' Kwin said, rinsing her hands in the river. 'Where were we?'

'Pranksy. You said, *technically*—'

'I was over the moon when that boy outed himself. Brave decision for someone so young, but when he asked my advice, I didn't mince words, Jim. You can't pretend to be someone you're not, I said, any more than you hide who you really are. Sit your parents down lad. Take a deep breath, then tell them straight out you're homo— *I can't.* Pranksy was frantic. *My dad'll kill me. He won't want a son who's homo*— He'll find out anyway, I said. Better he hears it from you that you're homo sapiens, than find out through gossip.'

'Are you saying his own father killed him?'

'What? No, of course not! Truth be told, his old man was proud of the way his boy came out, and like most of us, he was a huge fan.' She shot me a sharp sideways glance. 'How about you, Jim? Were you a fan of Pranksy's art?'

Seriously? Hunters spearing giant pink rats, with the slogan "Of Mice and Men"? Life-sized posters "Missing: Have you seen this Link?" Geese flying in an H formation "Illiteracy Rules"?

'Bet your jurassic park I was.'

His work was witty, clever, visionary even, and it made my heart sing that I'd been a cog in the creative wheel. But like I said, it was irreverent and the holy men were adamant. Stylised images? Tick. Deviation from the guidelines? Nope. Individuality? Not a chance in hell, however gifted. Which is why Pranksy sneaked out at night, and next morning another rock face would be sporting bright blue bison wearing boots with the caption "Meals on Heels."

But no more. That flame had been violently extinguished, and it scared me how we had no idea who among us was capable of such brutality.

The holy men? Or rather, someone acting on their behalf, stamping out the sacrilege once and for all?

The proverbial jealous lover? We all know how fame attracts girls like bees to honey, and my, did Banksy's blood run red in *that* department.

Or was the jealousy professional? A fellow artist, incensed at being constantly upstaged?

Watching Banky's pyre burn that night, I felt the heat of resentment burning hotter still. Spruce and Maple's efforts to unite the tribes through art was crumbling, as the paintbrush of suspicion pointed at everyone and no one. Trust blew away like Banksy's ashes on the wind.

My wife was right about needing to find the killer.

Still don't see why I should be saddled with the job.

• • • •

'TECHNICALLY WHAT?' The wife asked a week or so later.

'Technically what what?'

'You said the medicine woman found Pranksy's body outside her cave when she pulled aside the screen, and when you asked, was he killed there, she said *technically*—and that's as far as it went.'

Only because Kwin broke off yet again, this time to administer an anaesthetic to a patient who needed a tooth removed, and when I saw the sodding great boulder she selected, it seemed a good time to make an exit, and a rapid one at that.

'Apparently that's where he died, not where he was murdered.' I went back, of course. Just made sure I timed my visit for her lunch break. 'He was stabbed a hundred yards away and presumably left for dead, but somehow managed to crawl to the medicine woman.'

Hoping—praying—for help that didn't come.

'Poor, poor boy. Bleeding to death, all alone like that.' My wife sniffed into her squirrel skin hankie. 'Is it true, he wrote a giant V-sign in his own blood before he died?'

'Typical Pranksy.' I nodded. Swallowed the sadness. Forced a smile. 'Anti-establishment to the end.'

And then it hit me.

Not the rock Kwin used to knock out her dental patient.

Who killed Pranksy.

• • • •

'MY HERO!'

'Oh, Daddy, I'm so proud of you!'

'For he's a jolly good fellow...'

None of that happened, of course, but a man can dream. Plus there was satisfaction, knowing a killer no longer walked among us, brooding, invisible, dangerous and divisive.

Create a gap, though, and something always fills it. Before the swallows left in autumn, Pranksy's infamy had been eclipsed by the artist tasked to paint the holy cave with clouds and colourful figures, but who left the ceiling pristine. Mik Elangillo he's called. Something about modern art + blank canvas = free thinking, which roughly translates as "look at me", because that's all my daughters' generation want these days. Celebrity status.

Which, sad to say, was why Pranksy's life blood ended up ebbing away outside the medicine woman's cave.

Not even a fellow artist, which you could (perhaps) understand. The clash of new blood and fresh ideas, and all that other macho stuff young bucks deem necessary to prove their manhood. No, this was sour grapes pure and simple, and honestly. Can you think of a more tragic motive for taking someone's life?

The clue was the V-sign. Not a two-finger gesture at the establishment, as everybody thought. Pranksy was dying, and he knew it. With superhuman effort, he'd crawled to Kwin's cave, but either she slept too soundly to hear his cries for help or, more likely, he was too weak to call by then. With his last remaining breath, he named his killer.

'Bonjo?' My wife blinked in disbelief. 'The rock star?'

I didn't understand his popularity, myself. Dashing and good looking, yes, with his bouncy blond hair and athletic form. But where's the attraction in watching some bloke balanced on a tree trunk juggling stones while yodelling stuff like "Living with a Hare" and "You Give Doves A Bad Mane", eh?

'Fraid so, love.' I nodded towards where Plod was leading him away. 'Bonjo V.'

Took a life, simply because some upstart painter was getting more attention than his massive ego felt it deserved.

I turned to my wife. 'Remind me again why you sent me on that mission.'

Truly, I should have known better than to fish for compliments.

'Would you rather have a killer for a son-in-law?'

She had me at a total loss with that one.

'I thought Jagga might have murdered him. You know.' She clearly thought I did. 'The boy who's been courting our eldest for the past few weeks...?'

Between you and me, I wasn't sure my jaw would *ever* close.

'I was worried he was jealous, because she was two-timing him with Pranksy—'

'Our daughter's getting married?'

'Who do you think she was sending all those chippings to?'

Not sure which astonished me the most. My girl throwing her moleskin knickers at a graffiti artist. Or the fact that some idiot was daft enough to make her his woman.

I couldn't stop the tears from welling over. 'I'm going to pine.'

'Oh, Jimmy, sweetie, you'll get over it.'

'No, no, you don't understand,' I told my wife. 'I'm going to Pine, that's his tribe isn't it? Have a chat, chief to chief, make sure the contract's binding—' not giving that Jagga chance to change his bloody mind '—then straight home to celebrate.'

Sham pain. I love that stuff. The bit where I pretend to tap my wife on the head with my club, she giggles 'ow, ow, ow', then we fall in to bed.

Caveman? Maybe not such a mammoth job after all.

THE DAY OF THE JACKAL

Any setting sun, slanting through clouds, plays havoc with the shadows. Add on a Saxon church, an ancient graveyard, wobbly headstones and a line of dense, dark yew trees and imagination knows no bounds.

'Did you see that?'

The boy barely glanced up from his iPhone. 'See what?'

'The bloke at the lych gate, wearing a black animal mask.' The girl frowned. 'Kind of weird, don't you think?'

'Like a bank robber? Cool.' The boy spun round, aiming the phone's camera for a shot. Felt cheated when no one was there.

'Know what it reminded me of, all that black and gold?' The girl pulled up her collar, even though the evening was warm. 'Anubis.'

'A-who-bis?' For a hot second, he thought he caught a flash of movement from the corner of his eye. Pointed nose. Pricked-up ears. Except dogs weren't allowed in the graveyard unless they were on a leash.

'Like you weren't on that school trip to the Ashmolean Museum.' She landed a mock punch on his arm. 'Isis, Osiris, Hathor, Anubis. Ring a bell?'

'Riiiight. Head of a jackal, body of a man, Egyptian guide of the dead.' He remembered. Not because black symbolized the dark, fertile soil after the Nile floods subsided. Black was the colour of corpses after embalming. Double cool. 'Church drama's upped its game from Agatha Christie, then.'

'Anubis was the protector of graves,' she said, surprised the vicar's props ran to that level of detail. 'Tombs used to be sealed with his image.'

'So...some ancient Egyptian god, bored with the Valley of the the Kings, has taken to cruising English churchyards?'

'That's not what I meant and you know it, you idiot. Now give me half that Snickers bar, or it's the last time I do your English homework for you.'

'Yeah? Then who'd write your history projects?'

Their laughter echoed round the graveyard as the sun slid behind the steeple.

In the distance, a dog let out a single, haunting howl.

• • • •

'MISS EMMETT. WHAT A delightful surprise.'

'The feeling is mutual, Mr. Priest. Long time no see.' The jacket slipped from her shoulders and dropped on a chair. Her arms were toned, bare and tanned, and, like the red bandage dress and six-inch pencil heels, not the attire you normally associate with a funeral director's. 'What brings you to this quiet Sussex backwater, then?'

He ran his hand over his gleaming bald head, taking in her traffic-stopping legs, dark heavy curls, even darker flashing eyes, and a figure that hadn't changed in all the years he'd known her. 'Same as you, I imagine, Miss Emmett.'

He wanted to take his eyes off her, but dammit, that cleavage..

'Ah.' Her voice was so low, so slow, she practically purred. 'The temping agency sent you, too.'

'It appears the owner of this fine funeral home dined with his two sons in a restaurant that failed to follow the appropriate hygiene rules when it came to shellfish.'

'And since this is a family business—'

'—and his sons were the only employees—'

'—the firm was in urgent need of temporary staff.' She paused. 'What are the odds, do you think, of Daniel joining us on this one?'

'How many floating embalmers do you think there are in this country?' a voice drawled behind her.

'Mr. Wolfe.' Priest's smile was wide as he held out his hand. 'Delighted to be working with you again.'

'Likewise, Josh.' Dan returned the handshake, then leaned down to kiss Miss Emmett on her flawless cheek, catching a hint of her signature smoky perfume. 'You surprise me, Leonie. Still no ring on your finger?'

'Darling, please. I have my reputation as a man-eater to maintain.'

'I'd forgotten.' He laughed. 'Six husbands, as I recall, and none of them your own.'

'Make that seven.'

'Must be your lucky number, you're looking lovelier than ever. Wouldn't you agree, Josh?'

'Indeed I do, Mr. Wolfe. Ravishing would not be too strong a word, but.' The smile dropped from the little man's face. 'As much as I'd love to catch up, I think this is best done over dinner tonight. Apparently the Fox & Hounds does an excellent beef and ale pie. But for now, we have a body to prepare, and very little time in which to do it.'

'Whose?' Dan asked.

'White male, twenty-eight years of age, a welder by the name of—' He consulted the white board on the wall listing the deceased's height, weight, clothing, date of passing, as well as their personal effects '—Ryan Williams.'

'Car crash?' Leonie asked.

'Stab wounds to the chest and stomach, Miss Emmett. Neither of which, might I add, were self-inflicted.'

For a moment, the only sound in the undertaker's mortuary was the whirr of the refrigerated unit's fan, keeping its occupants comfy at a constant three degrees.

Dan flicked through the register. 'According to this, the funeral's tomorrow, with viewings in the Chapel of Rest starting four p.m. today.'

'Like I said, Mr. Wolfe. A narrow window in which to work, and little chance to...correct any errors.'

'In which case.' Miss Emmett's smile was sultry, yet no less genuine as she handed her folically challenged colleague a box of latex gloves. 'The sooner we set to work, gentlemen, the better.'

• • • •

IF YOU'VE NEVER BEEN inside an undertaker's mortuary (and how many of us have?), it's a cross between a dentist's, a doctor's examination room, and your dad's old garden shed. In other words, a lot of stainless steel, masses of towels, sheets, wires and tubes, as well as sterilizing equipment, sinks, shelves displaying more liquid sprays than the average supermarket, assorted buckets, bins and trays, along with several odd-looking bits of machinery that could pass for breadmakers, microwaves, blenders or wall-heaters. But which in fact drain the blood from the body and replace it with embalming fluid.

'Williams... Williams...' Dan frowned as he opened the top drawer of the triple refrigeration unit. 'Why does that name ring a bell?'

'Perhaps, Mr. Wolfe—' the undertaker tossed him the local newspaper, open at page five '—because he was arrested for killing his married lover by throwing her down the stairs after she broke off the affair. Ryan claimed he was innocent, don't they all, but the lady's husband held a somewhat different opinion. While the police were escorting Mr. Williams from his apartment to the car, he lunged at him with a kitchen knife and this, my friends.' Priest's mouth twisted as he removed the sheet from Ryan's body in preparation for embalming. 'This is the result.'

'Either wound would have killed him.'

'The husband was ex-army. No hesitation, no doubts, straight for the kill.'

'In-te-res-ting.' Leonie stretched out the word to a musical rhythm. 'Because according to our employer's notes here, the wife sustained fractures and bruises consistent with being thrown down the stairs. But at the bottom, underlined in red ink no less, he quotes the police report, which states the cause of death as a clean break to the neck.'

Dan looked at her. She looked at Priest. Priest looked at the young man on the fibreglass tray.

'When people ask, why do I do what I do for a living,' Dan said. 'I joke that it's because the dead don't talk back.' He paused. 'The hell they bloody don't.'

These weren't mere corpses being prepared for their journey. Here was somebody's father, cut down by a heart attack. Somebody's wife, taken by ice on a bend in the road. A toddler, drowned in a garden pond. A grandfather, who had lived and loved and danced and cried. A boy, whose unformed teenage frontal lobe told him life wasn't worth living after she dumped him.

The life force had gone, but these people were not diminished by death. And when you're massaging their limbs, to make sure the out-flow of blood and in-flow of embalming fluid is one and the same, or plugging the holes in their abdomen where you drained out their viscera, you're talking unimaginable intimacy.

This is when the dead talk to you.

Some stories they're happy for everyone to hear, through laughter lines, piercings, tans and tattoos. But when you open an artery and find it clogged with cholesterol, or cut into the body and smell alcohol, or find the hidden scars of self-harm cuts and burns, they're telling you their deepest, darkest secrets.

Ryan Williams had no secrets.

The only scars he carried were typical welder spark and spatter burns, and even these were old. The learning curve of an apprenticeship. No tattoos. No piercings. The lines round his mouth and eyes curled upwards.

While the machines gurled and pumped, trickled and drained, Dan considered the piece in the paper. In particular, the part where Ryan insisted she was leaving her husband, not ending the affair. Swore blind, in fact, they were planning to start a new life together. Raise a family.

'Contrast the face on this tray with the face on page five,' Dan said. 'What do you see?'

'Mouth pursed, eyes hard, even in army fatigues.' Leonie's hands somehow remained elegant, even in latex gloves. 'The husband has bully-boy written all over him.'

'Probably why the army threw him out,' Mr. Priest said. 'Doubtless further fuelling his alpha male complex.'

'Turning him, say, into the sort who can't handle rejection?' Dan murmured.

'The if-I-can't-have-her-no-one-else-can type?' Leonie suggested. 'The sort of man who, no way, would let his wife's lover get the better of him?'

'Exactly.' Dan switched off the machines. 'He throws his wife down the stairs, finishes her off with a well-trained snap of the neck, and in doing so, neatly frames the boyfriend.'

'Hold hard, Mr. Wolfe. The police would have looked very, very closely at the husband.'

'Which is why he took himself off the suspect list by killing Ryan in that convincing act of grief-stricken revenge.'

'Then we should go to the police,' Leonie said. 'The three of us together, and report our conclusions as a team.'

'She's right, Mr. Wolfe. The more statements, the more weight to the argument.'

'Ryan's not going anywhere, Dan. This can wait, whereas the quicker that bastard pays—'

'Sorry, this can't wait.' Dan pointed to the clock on the wall. 'Ryan's parents are coming down for a viewing, and we owe it to them that their son looks as close in his coffin as to when he was alive.'

'Straight after they've gone, then,' Leonie said, reaching for the make-up. 'The world needs to know they're burying an innocent man. The family, if nothing else, deserves that.' As did Ryan. 'We can't let the bastard get away with it, Josh.'

'Justice will prevail, Miss Emmett, I have every confidence. Don't you agree, Mr. Wolfe?'

Daniel thought of the knife wounds in the young welder's chest. The first to kill. The second just to be nasty.

'What goes around comes around,' he said quietly.

All the same, it saddened him beyond measure to see another bright flame snuffed out.

· · · ·

IT'S A POPULAR MISCONCEPTION that embalming preserves every corpse like Lenin's. Quite frankly, unless you're Pharoah, with seventy days to spare and unlimited public funds, the closest you'll ever get to your own pyramid is a Toblerone. For the most part, embalming is one of many processes designed to achieve that famous "just sleeping" look, so that when family and friends say their final goodbyes, the memory they take with them is a good one.

But like writers who take twenty years to become an overnight success, or supermodels who appear so effortlessly beautiful in magazine shoots, a lot of hard graft goes in to making it happen. Guiding Ryan Williams' parents through their harrowing ordeal, Daniel wondered how they'd feel, if they knew funeral directors shot wire into their clients' jawbones and septum, to keep the mouths centred and closed. Or that little spiked caps were placed over the eyes, which attached themselves to the eyelids to make sure they stayed closed. Or the level of skill required in applying make-up that makes the dead look exactly how they were in life.

But Ryan's loved ones had bigger issues to deal with.

His parents? Brought to their knees, because they hadn't done something—anything—to protect their only son. His sisters? Devastated that it had been a week, nearer two, since they last spoke. His work mates and friends? Eaten alive by the loss.

Every last one tortured by the knowledge that they never got chance to say goodbye. Or tell him how much he meant to them.

• • • •

'HERE.'

'What's that?'

'What does it look like? A whole Snickers bar. You deserve it.'

They were walking through the churchyard, the boy and the girl, but a whole day had passed since the man in the mask, and in England the rain rarely keeps off for long. Although the drizzle had stopped, at least for a while, the path was more puddles than paving slabs, and there was very little sun to slant through the clouds.

'What for?' the girl asked.

'Your history project. Talk about cool. All that stuff about Anubis standing over the priest during the embalming, then guiding the dead to the Halls of Justice, where their hearts are weighed against the feather of truth? Whoa.'

'Ostrich feather,' the girl added proudly.

'And then, if they passed the test—what was it he did?'

'You mean the Opening of the Mouth?'

The ceremony in which jackal-headed Anubis opens not only their mouth and their nostrils, but also their eyes, that they might see, breathe and talk with their ancestors in the Land of the Reeds.

'Beats the shit out of the stuff I knocked out for you, about William of Orange and Disraeli and Cromwell. In fact, you can have my Pringles, as well, if you like.'

Why not? She wasn't allowed junk food at home, and there's only so much broccoli a fifteen-year-old can take.

'Tell you what would be really cool,' she said, crunching. 'To see the look on the face of that scumbag from Bartley Street, when it's time for *his* heart to be weighed.'

'The bloke who snapped his wife's neck—*crack!*—like a chicken, then tried to pin the blame on the boyfriend?'

It was all over the local news channels at breakfast. Something to do with snorting a bad batch of M-CAT, inducing paranoid fears of monsters coming to get him, so that when the police turned up to question him, he blabbed every last detail, right down to things only the killer would know.

Of course, he tried to retract the confession once his teeth had stopped grinding. Said he never took drugs, never heard of M-CAT, someone must have slipped it in his drink in the Fox & Hounds last night.

Tough.

Forensic evidence spoke for itself. He was going down for double murder.

'Thought he was clever.' The boy jumped a puddle. 'But in the end, these types are never as tough as they like to make out, and I bet, when his heart gets weighed, he cries like a baby. *Oh, please, Anubis! Please don't throw me in the Lake of Fire...*'

'He will, though.' The girl pulled the Snickers apart, and handed half to her friend. 'The jackal will toss his black heart to Ammit.'

'Who's Emmett?'

'Ammit, you idiot! She's only the goddess of divine retribution.'

'Riiiight.' Head of a crocodile, body of a lion, hindquarters of a hippo. 'Ugliest woman on earth.'

'The most terrifying,' she corrected. 'Ammit represented everything the Egyptians feared most, their three largest predators rolled into one. And when hearts were judged bad, Anubis tossed them to Ammit the man-eater, who gobbled them up and made sure their souls never found peace.'

'Dunno where you got all that stuff from, but I'm glad you did.' The boy cocked his head on one side. 'You'll still do my maths homework, though, right?'

They were still laughing when she pushed him into the puddle.

THE GIRL WHO WALKED ON ROOFTOPS

'Seriously?'

'Seriously.'

'If I was able to walk across any rooftops in the world, which city would I choose?'

We were sitting in the interview room. Me, DC Wood, some bearded solicitor and, of course, Janice. I suppose, with hindsight, I shouldn't have been surprised by the question, having known her since we were eight and a half, when she skipped into the classroom halfway through the spring term, took the spare desk next to mine as if she'd sat there all her life, then promptly started drawing in the margins of her books. Devils, dragons, sabre-tooth tigers and trolls. Mum always said she'd turn out wrong.

'Janice, there's a man lying the morgue with a barcode instead of a coffin—'

'Kenny Bates.' She shrugged. 'No great loss to society.'

To say I found her indifference shocking was an understatement. 'Maybe so, but we still need to talk about what happened.'

'Humour me,' she said, and there it was. The smile that lit up rooms and won everybody over. The smile my mother told me not to trust, because when you've been shunted from foster home to foster home, you soon learn to play people.

That girl's going to end up in jail, you mark my words.

In this soulless little room I could almost hear Mum's voice, and bless her, right up to when her liver failed, she still believed that being born during that hippy-Woodstock-chill-man-peace thing made it OK for her and Dad to fight like pitbulls in a cage. That it was BoHo chic for her only child to clear piles of food-encrusted plates from the sink because her mother was passed out on the stairs, dead drunk. Again. And wade through dirty laundry for something that might, just might, pass as clean to wear for school. But she loved me and looked out for me, and so did Dad. It was just that his work in dam construction took him away for weeks at a time, when he did come home, his neck smelled of a different woman's perfume every time. Consequently, dysfunction was the glue that bound chalk and cheese together. Janice and I became the sisters neither of us had ever had.

But that was thirty years ago.

The world had changed.

I had changed.

The smile no longer fooled me.

'If you could walk across any rooftops in the world,' she said, still lighting up the room, goddammit, 'which city would you choose?'

I shot DC Wood a conspiratorial glance. Long, long, long ago, Woody and I were raw recruits together at the police training college, Hendon. The difference was, I was ambitious and couldn't wait to ditch the uniform. A decade passed before he made detective constable.

'Paris.'

'Oh, me too!' She clapped her hands together like a little child. 'What a weekend, eh? Did we paint that town red or what!'

Like bats from a cave, the memories came flying. Climbing the Eiffel Tower. Riding the Métro. A cruise down the Seine. Our first taste of *foie gras*, our first brush with *pastis*, eating chicken from the *rôtisserie* on the corner. More exciting memories, too. Sipping wine at pavement cafés in Montmartre. Dancing till dawn. Two lost virginities. Never mind that sabre-tooth tiger tattoo...

'We most certainly did.'

'For years after,' Janice said, 'you told me that was the best time of your life.'

'It was,' I said truthfully.

'Mine, too, for all we'd just turned seventeen.'

She sighed, and suddenly I knew neither of us were in this room with its cameras and tape recorders, and its ugly photos, spread out on the table, of a hideously misshapen body. We were kids again, getting into scrapes, talking our way out of them—nothing vicious, malicious, nothing particularly wild. Just testing the boundaries, playing if-only, doing everything in our power to escape the hell that was home.

How—why—did we ever lose touch?

'Tell me,' she whispered. 'Tell me what you see when you walk across the rooftops of Paris. Let me live it again. Please. One last time...'

'Very well.' I closed my eyes. Didn't *dare* look at Woody. 'I'm skipping over chimneys, slates and pantiles with my sunglasses perched on top my head, counting the bridges over the Seine, the fountains round the Eiffel Tower, the theatrical masks that ring the Opéra's bright green copper dome. Down there's our narrow little hotel, painted pink with green shutters—'

'Is the paint still peeling off?'

'In bloody great sweeps.' Despite myself, I laughed. 'Now I'm twirling above the Sacré Coeur—'

'Remember we pretended it was the Taj Mahal?'

'And laughed at all those poor sods wheezing up the steps, while we shinned like monkeys?'

Those were the days...

'No, no, don't stop,' Janice begged. 'Not yet. What else do you see?'

For Chrissakes, what harm could it do? 'Now I'm perched between the twin bell towers of Notre Dame, looking at the spire.'

'What about the gargoyles? Are they still there?'

'Beaked, horned and crouching with menace,' I said, 'while traffic horns blast round the Arc de Triomphe—'

'Can you see our reflections in the shops along the Champs Elysées?'

'Like a mirror, along with that horrid C4 that we broke into and ate chips in the back seat, pretending it was ours, and of course the red sails of the Moulin Rouge.'

Oh, my, were those the days!

'Good,' Janice said crisply. 'I'm glad you'll have some happy memories, walking those rooftops. Life sentences do tend to drag.'

My eyes jerked open. *Prison?*

'What? You didn't think I knew you killed him?'

'Me?' My head was spinning. 'I didn't kill anyone. You asked me to come down to the station, to help fill in some background on Kenny Morton, because he was an ex-boyfriend back in the day. Well, here I am.'

'With your solicitor.' She shot a sharp glance at the man who'd been taking copious notes.

'A precaution,' I said.

'And a good one, because I know, and DC Wood knows, that you pushed Kenny Morton off the roof of his apartment building, isn't that right, DC Woods?'

'Yes, Ma'am.'

'You really should have stuck the training course out,' Janice said, 'or at least kept up to speed with advances in forensics.'

'He committed suicide. You said.' I turned to her stony-faced subordinate. 'Back me up here, Woody. She said Kenny jumped—'

'The Inspector's words,' he quoted from his notebook, 'were that *it appeared that Kenny jumped*.'

I didn't like the way he emphasised the word "appeared".

'Clever girl, you wore gloves,' Janice said, 'but you should have put them on in the street, not in the lift. We found partial prints inside, and on the button in the lobby.'

She was bluffing. I knew this woman inside out. She was bloody bluffing.

'We also have the text you sent him, asking to meet you on the roof, and please don't look at me like that. Drug dealers run a lot of phones, you took them all, but you didn't take into account that the one you texted him on was his personal number, not pay-as-you-go. We traced the exchange of texts, and if you remember, back in Paris, when we were up the Eiffel Tower, do you know what you said?'

'Isn't the view lovely?'

'You said, it would be so easy to kill someone by pushing them off a roof. All they had to do was trust you.'

'Jesus, Janice, that was twenty years ago!'

'Lucky for Kenny Morton I have a good memory.'

'This is bollocks. We broke up five, six years ago, and I ended it, not him, so I can hardly have been holding some kind of jilted lover grudge.'

'If you're asking me, I don't think you've loved anyone in your life, and maybe your solicitor can pass that on to your QC to use in your defence? Citing your drunk of a mother, your philandering father. Child abuse, even indirect, does leave a scar.'

I had no intention of rising to her bait. 'I had absolutely no motive for killing Kenny Morton, so unless you intend to—'

'Cannabis.' This was DC Woods. 'You were lazy at Hendon, that's why they tossed you out, you haven't held a job down longer than a month in twenty years, and you were looking for an easy way to make money.'

'I had no idea Kenny was involved—'

'He was growing it when you two were an item.' Janice ticked the points off on her fingers. 'You knew the business was still going strong. You wanted in. And when he said no—'

'Wisely, in my opinion,' Woody murmured.

'—you killed him for no other reason than spite.'

All those times growing up. Getting into scrapes. Talking ourselves out of them.

It wasn't over yet...

'You said yourself, Kenny was no great loss to society.'

'He wasn't,' Janice said. 'Any more than you. But he *is* a loss to his mother and three sisters, not to mention a father, who had a heart attack and is intensive care now, thanks to you.'

In the distance, words were buzzing in the air like bees. Something about arresting me for the murder of... may harm my defence... later rely on in court...

But all I could hear was Janice. Asking, if I could walk across any rooftops in the world, which city would I choose?

THE OLD MAN AND THE SEASHORE

E yes that were once blacker than night were now cloudy. Hands that used
to wring a chicken's neck in one snap merely quivered. Corded muscles
hung slack.

They used to be afraid of him.

Children.

The big man, living in the blue painted shack on the shore.

Jules le Géant, they called him.

Jules the Giant.

In the early days, when he first took up residence on the edge of town,
arriving in his shabby little boat with just one even shabbier suitcase and a bag
slung across his shoulder, a group of them, mostly boys, would creep up, dare
one of the number to shin over the fence, knock on his door, and then run.

This only happened three or four times. The next time he heard them
sniggering, ssssshhhhing, building up the bravado, he was ready. When the first
knuckle rapped, he flung the door open and roared at the top of his lungs.
Occasionally, some of the older boys would taunt him with chants. But only at
night, and on the public side of the fence. What they did over there was none
of his business, he ignored them. After a while, the children stopped coming.

'Where's he from, Henri?'

'What do you know about him?'

'Why did he come here, to Barras?'

Short, thickset, with dark wavy hair and eyebrows that met over the bridge
of his nose, Henri Grimaud was the most powerful man between here and
La Rochelle. As mayor of the town, he was both the elected authority in the
commune, and the State's representative in it. He set and managed the budget,
was responsible for preserving local heritage, conservation of the environment
and the issue of building permits, as well as being in charge of public health
and safety, social issues, and local administration. He officated at weddings,
was registrar of births and deaths, and was entitled to special powers under
the authority of the public prosecutor for the repression of crime. To admit he
hadn't a clue was unthinkable.

'I am not at liberty to say,' he'd reply stiffly.

In a country where bureaucracy reigned supreme and required dozens of forms to be filled in, in triplicate naturally, the mayor knew precisely when and where Duplessis was born. July 17th, 1948, a fishing village in Brittany. He knew the names of his parents, both long since dead, that Jules had a sister, Marie-Christine, and his trade was listed as carpenter, even though no one had ever seen him work wood or use tools. *Monsieur le Maire* was also aware that Jules Duplessis had left Brittany forty years earlier. What he'd done, and where he'd been, before he washed up in Barras, was a mystery. Even with all those damned forms.

'If you want to know more, you'll have to ask him yourself,' he would add, knowing full well that nobody would.

So. While the rest of Barras went about its business, raising succulent oysters and fat, juicy mussels to ship to Paris, Bordeaux and Lyon, or running hotels and restaurants, or growing fruit and vegetables to sell in the market, or baking hot, flaky croissants and bread sold by the kilo, *Jules le Géant* kept himself to himself, combing the beach after each tide and selling his finds to the tourists who flocked here in the summer for the endless dunes and gorgeous rocky coves, and a sun that never seemed to set.

The tide was a generous benefactor. It donated shells, driftwood, starfish and cuttlefish bones, as you'd expect, along with all manner of flotsam and jetsam, ranging from ropes and chains and other boating equipment to beads and bones, flyswatters, rubber ducks and, once, a metre-and-a-half tall plastic snowman.

One reason Barras was so suited to the mollusc industry was that it was wrapped around a mass of tiny inlets, cuts, streams and canals. All tidal. All ripe for a beachcomber's pickings.

Also, the cliffs themselves weren't very high—two or three metres, no more—but the rocks below were unusual. Like the Giant's Causeway in Ireland (how appropriate), they resembled large cobblestones, and the *Golfe de Gascogne*, what English visitors called Biscay, wasn't famous for its tranquil nature. In winter, February in particular, wild storms swept in from the Atlantic to batter the coast, and often, after a heavy tidal surge, the good folk of Barras would wake up to find another cobblestone gone. Left behind in the holes was anything too heavy, too awkard or too pointy to wash out again. Irons, pans and gears lodged and became trapped, along with anchors, daggers, dumb bells, tyres. Statues of the Virgin Mary were unaccountably common.

With ten full months between the end of one tourist season and the beginning of the next, Jules' collection of chipped, dented, barnacle-encrusted objects grew to the point where it not longer fitted under the awning that ran along the back of his fence, but spread across the rough patch of ground that passed for a garden, virtually encroaching on the cracked, narrow path that led to his door. Honestly, you wouldn't believe what people forget, abandon, discard or simply lose after a day on the beach. Toys, sneakers, blouses, umbrellas, mugs, picnic baskets, towels, necklaces, bracelets and rings, to name but a few.

But you know what they say.

One man's junk is another man's keepsake.

It's amazing what people buy, when they're having fun.

• • • •

'IS THIS A NARWHAL TOOTH?'

Jules glanced round from his *baguette*. With her thick blonde hair, white blouse and cut-off jeans, the girl seemed vaguely familiar.

'Yes.'

Twisted pipe, narwhal tooth, what did it matter? By the time someone pointed out the mistake, assuming anyone did, she'd be miles away, in Rouen or Limoges, or wherever these people came from. Leaning with his back against the wall, he carried on munching.

'How much is it?'

'5€.'

'Sounds cheap. They must be common round here.'

On a scale of one to a hundred, whales from the Arctic Circle ranked as are-you-taking-the-piss.

'Fairly.'

He sliced off another chunk of *saucisson sec* and balanced it on his *baguette*. That little snub nose. Definitely familiar, but he still couldn't place her. Most likely a tourist from last year, back to explore the mussel beds or feast on the oysters. Back end of September, with the air calm and the sun's strength still fierce, they were coming into their own. A feature restaurateurs took advantage of, remaining open right through the year. Unlike most coastal resorts, when the shutters came down the first day the schools went back, turning the place into a ghost town.

'This is pretty.'

The girl had abandoned the lump of old pipe in favour of a blue china pig, painted with tiny pink flowers. Not every item on sale had been washed up or forgotten. After the locals became aware of his collection, they began turning up with armfuls of unwanted china, glassware, all manner of bric-a-brac. Jules never bought. He wasn't in this for the money. All he needed was enough to get by, keep his head down, and not have to mix. Perhaps they felt sorry for him, this big, shambling recluse? Perhaps they were curious? Perhaps they were too lazy to take their damn junk to the tip. Either way, some of the locals had taken to leaving various bits and bobs at the gate. Perhaps they meant well? Who cares.

'2€.'

Sell stuff cheap enough, and cash soon starts to stack up.

'My sister and I used to have piggy banks like this, when we were little.'

This was an ornament, not a piggy bank. He chewed on his sausage. Pulled off another chunk of *baguette*.

'Clear plastic ours were, though, with a competition for whose filled up the quickest.' The girl's smile was wistful. 'I won hands down every time, but I wish now I hadn't.' She put the china pig back where she'd found it. 'I'd cheat, by swapping larger denominations for heaps of centimes.'

Having eaten enough, big hands carefully wrapped the *saucisson* back in its greaseproof paper, sealing the remainder of the *baguette* in a linen bag, to keep it fresh to feed to the gulls. Leave bread in the open air round here, and in an hour's time it's harder than—well, narwhal teeth.

'I got away with it, see, because she's four years younger than me.' Blue eyes filled with tears. 'Arlette. That's her name, you know. Arlette.'

He took a swig of cider. *Brut*. Couldn't stand the sweet stuff. Wiped his hands down the sides of his trousers.

'The house is off limits.'

She looked surprised, and he couldn't decide whether it was because he'd jolted her out of her own little world, or because he'd referred to the tumbledown shack as a house.

'Is it? Sorry.'

There were hundreds, correction, thousands of cabins like this around here, lining the canals, edging the inlets, all with some kind of mooring for boats. Some stood on stilts, some were stone built, but most of them were timber constructions with tiled pitched roofs, all of them bigger than they appeared from the outside. Oystermen's cabins. A feature of the region and a photographer's dream, being brightly painted and every one so utterly different from its neighbour. Orange with green doors and blue windows. Blue with canary yellow doors and red windows. Pale pink with red doors, dark blue, light blue, red stripes, two-tone, ramshackle, rustic, chic. Some were beside jetties, others next to pontoons and piers, and others, like Jules', isolated with just a post in the water to tie up to. Although uninhabited for the most part, some owners grew tall spikes of hollyhocks at the front, or planters bursting with sweet-scented herbs. A few of the cabins had been lovingly decorated with murals, a few more turned into gift shops, and one enterprising soul had actually linked four together, to form a restaurant with a terrace at the edge of the water.

Flat bottomed boats constantly chugged up and down the channels, bringing in baskets of oysters to serve with white wine, crusty bread and a lemon. The smell of salt carried heavy on the breeze. Gulls screamed as they wheeled overhead.

'Only I thought I saw some crucifixes among the clutter inside.'

'It's not clutter.' Jules snapped the door shut. 'That's stock I haven't got round to cleaning up.'

Maybe she was a day-tripper, who'd stopped by once before, and that's how he knew her? Lord knows, they were plentiful enough. Artists, attracted by the views to Fort Boyard out at sea. Walkers, hiking the open coastal path. Casual diners, stopping for *moules frites* in one of the many waterside restaurants. Like summer tourists, a lot of them liked to pick up a souvenir before heading home, and back to work the next day.

'One of the crucifixes looked shiny and new.'

'Things get dropped.'

'Shouldn't you hand them in to the police?'

'Why? Teaches people to be more careful in future. Are you buying that?'

'What would I want with a garden gnome that's lost its fishing rod?' The snub nose wrinkled in distaste. 'I'll take the china pig, though.'

'3€.'

'I thought you said two.'

'Three.'

An extra euro for wasting his time.

'She went missing.' The girl dug out a five euro note. 'Arlette.'

'Two change.'

'Last summer it was.' She rubbed the pig's back, as though for good luck. 'Barras was the last place she was seen.'

'Holiday romance most like. Or run off with one of the gypsies. They're fine looking boys.'

'That's what the police said. *Probably backpacking round Australia right this moment,* they said. *Having a whale of a time.*'

'They know what they're talking about.'

'I suppose so.' She stared at the pig. 'Only...Arlette wasn't like that. Why would she go off without letting me know?'

Jules stared at the big, shambling shadow on the side of the hut, and said nothing. What, after all, was there to say?

'Our parents died in a crash five years ago. All we have is each other.'

'She's young. Young people are impulsive.'

'The police said that, too.' The girl blew into a tissue. '*See it all the time,* they said. *Students working the summer to pay for university. Itinerant lifestyle becomes seductive. They meet like-minded souls, lose track of time, think keeping in touch doesn't matter.*'

Feeling that he was expected to make some reply, Duplessis grunted.

'They asked, *how long before she disappeared since you spoke?*' She flicked her blonde hair over her shoulder. 'Like four or five weeks meant we weren't close! Of course Arlette followed the work! We both did. Sometimes it was the vineyards, sometimes waiting tables, but we kept in touch, when we could.'

'You'd have heard, if there was bad news.'

'So everyone tells me. Bad news travels fast. But I thought...If I came here... Saw where she worked, talked to people she mixed with...' Her face clouded. 'The trouble is, no one remembers Ailette. Not clearly.'

'It was high season. Not like today.'

In July and August, the town was overrun with thousands, literally thousands, of tourists—and thousands of tourists meant casual labour, all paid in cash, no questions asked, and no records.

He shrugged. 'Employers can't be expected to keep track of every kid who passes through.'

'I know. It was a long shot, I understand that, but I still had to take it.' She patted the garish china ornament. 'Thanks for your time.'

'Hm.'

He watched her close the gate behind her. Sure he'd seen her somewhere before...

'Here.'

He tossed her a euro coin, which she caught.

'You were right. The pig cost two euros, not three.'

• • • •

SUNSET. ANOTHER REASON why artists and photographers flocked to the Atlantic coast. The incredible spectacle of nature, reddening the sky, colouring the cliffs, turning the sea to molten copper. Terns made their last dives of the day for fish. Bats squeaked on the wing. Gulls flapped languidly across the fiery horizon to their roost.

Jules the Giant sighed.

Soon, the cranes and the storks would be heading south again. The hoopoes would be on their way to Africa, ditto the warblers and the swallows, and before long the first slight chill of autum would creep in to the evening air.

He listened to the waves washing soft against the shoreline. Waves that brought him gifts on every tide, and, with them, the freedom to be himself and do the things he liked to do. Accountable to no one. Responsible for nothing. Obligated to nobody but himself.

This was how it had always been. The big awkward man, who had been the big awkward kid at school.

An outsider then.

An outsider now.

He wouldn't have it any other way.

As the sun dipped and the sky darkened, Duplessis remained motionless, staring across the ocean into space. The only sounds were the wind singing in the dunes, and the gentle splash of lapping water, hypnotic and comforting.

The garden had become so overgrown with junk that it was on the cusp of becoming a talking point. A quirky landmark for tourists to check out, an object of curiosity for curiosity's sake. He'd seen it happen before.

Too many people.

Too much talk.

This was the end of the season in every sense.

Duplessis waited until the light faded. Inside his shack, he flicked on a light and pulled his suitcase down from the shelf. Like the first hint of autumn, old age was also creeping up. Arms that used to lift three times his body weight without breaking sweat could barely lift half that, these days. Hands that could lock a vice-like grip for twenty minutes just about managed ten. Where he'd been able to haul on the oars all day long, if he'd needed, was reduced to three hours at best.

Stacking his meagre possessions into the case, he had no regrets. Change was inevitable, especially for drifters. Jules lived life his way, on his own terms. How many men could say that?

Boots, papers, sweaters, vests. He was an expert at packing, never sorry to leave when it became time to move on.

Clearing space on the *clic-clac* that doubled as sofa and bed, he picked up the crucifix.

'Of course.'

That's why the girl looked familiar.

In his giant paw, the necklace seemed lost.

He remembered her now. Same snub nose, but brown hair, not blonde. Not quite as skinny, either, and her eyes, they weren't blue. No, no. They were green. Jules remembered exactly how green they were, bulging with terror as his hands closed round her throat. Again, and again, and again.

He picked up the box he kept next to his pillow. Inside were fifty-eight other necklaces. Mementoes of his travels around the French coast.

Well, well, well. Who'd have thought it. The sister, eh?

Jules climbed into his little boat and shipped the oars.

True, he couldn't do all the things today that he used to. But as long as he had the strength to wrap chains round their young, naked bodies and dump them way out at sea, life was good.

Silently, the rope slipped from its mooring post.

Maybe, God willing, he'd bump into the sister again some time?

That was a mighty pretty opal that hung round her neck.

M ost marble merchants, even third generation with the business handed to them on a plate, still like to drink from the fountain of knowledge. Cassius Gallus was considered lucky if he gargled twice a week, and that was fine by Claudia. Better than fine, in fact. She considered lack of intellect his best asset.

Tall, dark and really rather handsome in a round-faced, softish sort of way, he was wealthy, honest, trusting as a puppy. The ideal match for young widows, obliged by law to re-marry within two years of their husband's death.

'Swear on your mother's life, Leonides, are you absolutely sure?'

'Yes, madam.' Her lanky Macedonian steward nodded solemnly. Then again, solemn was the only emotion he knew. 'I am absolutely sure.'

Today was New Year's Day, the start of three days' non-stop revelry, and the perfect time to propitiate the gods, Janus in particular, to guarantee good luck throughout the coming year. With her marriage coming up in just a few weeks, Claudia wasn't taking chances. Not a hot damn single one.

'You've dotted extra lamps round the house, each filled to the brim with scented oil?'

Lights to roll in a year full of brightness. Clove oil to thwart adverse influences, honeysuckle for prosperity, almond, sage and basil for success—and so what tonight's guests would need pegs on their noses? The advantages more than outweighed any gagging.

'You've brought in sweetmeats and honey like I asked?'

'*By the barrowload* was the term I believe you used.'

Excellent. The diners might get sick, they might get fat, they will definitely break out in pimples, but sweet things represent peace. Especially by the barrowload.

'You've polished up the gold and silver, and set every piece around the place to catch the light and gleam?'

Leonides nodded in a way that suggested Claudia's guests would be blinded while they were throwing up from sweetmeat overload, but heavy metals attract prosperity. A girl can't have too much of that.

'And we have sufficient laurel branches in the house?'

'We have, madam.'

'Especially the dining hall and atrium?'

'Enough to make me fear for the next three years' crowning ceremonies.'

Must be New Year, if Leonides was cracking jokes.

'Excellent. Well done.' With everything crossed off the list, Claudia snapped her wax tablet shut, leaned back in her chair and folded her arms. 'The porter has his instructions. Make sure he follows them to the letter.'

The first person to enter determines the category of fortune for the coming year. Women with red or fair hair are guaranteed to bring bad luck, but she wasn't jinxing this wedding. *Not one single female foot across that threshold*, she'd told the porter, *even if you have to chain every woman to the gatepost*. At least until Cassius arrived, which—she glanced at the shadow of the sun dial in the peristyle—would be any minute now. Oh yes. Claudia rubbed her hands. Tall, dark-haired men were just the ticket to ensure good fortune for the next twelve months, and insurance policies don't come any better than third generation marble merchants, with the business handed to them on a plate.

She dabbed a splash of perfume in her collar bones. Fiddled with her necklace, bracelet, rings and ear rings, making sure each displayed just-so. Shook her shimmering pale peach gown so that it half-covered her feet and showed off her pretty new gilded sandals. Added a smidge more kohl around her eyes, enough to make them smoulder without overdoing things, and decided the only thing left now was count her blessings. Was any abacus in the Empire big enough?

Time passed. No Cassius. More time passed. Perhaps she should have a word with the porter? Because if he'd got it back to front and chained her future husband to the gatepost, she'd hang his leathery little gizzards round his neck and— Ah! Deep voices rumbling in the atrium! Irritation was immediately supplanted by a warm glow of satisfaction. Only slightly marred by the fact that she hadn't ordered the lamps to be lit in the morning, so how come she smelled sandalwood? And who took it upon themselves to add that particular oil, when it wasn't on the—?

Every blessing she'd been counting dropped down dead.

This wasn't her tall, dark insurance policy ushering in a year's good luck. Hell, no. This was the Security Police, looking like it had swallowed a sea urchin whole and half the spines were still stuck in his mouth.

. . . .

'MARCUS CORNELIUS ORBILIO. What a delightful surprise.'

Janus, Janus, Janus, what in the name of all the gods did I do to piss you off? Didn't I sacrifice enough wine? Feed you enough spelt and salt cakes? Sprinkle enough saffron on the hearth? Dammit, she'd burned enough incense at the altar to choke a dozen camels, *and* she'd sacrificed to Janus before any other god this morning. What more did the two-headed bastard want?

Dredging up the widest smile in the universe, Claudia was about to thank the Security Police for dropping by, then point out (ever so politely, of course) that by some inexplicable error he wasn't on tonight's guest list, and what a pity because it was too late to re-arrange the seating plan, when more deep voices rumbled in the atrium.

'My, aren't you in for fantastic luck!' If Cassius had a tail, he'd be wagging it. 'Two dark-haired men first-footing at the same time, what are the odds, eh?'

What indeed, and as for Janus. Two faces or not, she would punch both of them when this was over.

'Sorry I'm late, darling, only the weirdest thing happened on the Capitol as I was coming here. You know today's the day when magistrates—or is it consuls? or maybe praetors? some kind of politicians anyway have their inauguration, and everyone's gathered at Jupiter's temple to...well, whatever it is they do at these ceremonies, before they sacrifice a pure white heifer. Or is it a bull? or an ox? Beside the point. You'll never guess what happened!'

He never gave her the chance, every word was running into one, and credit where it's due. He was ace at breath control.

'Just as the bull...heifer...ox thingy was being led towards the altar, beautifully decked out, I have to say, gilded horns, gorgeous garlands, sacred sash, the lot—anyway, before the acolytes had chance to hobble it, can you believe some joker shot it with an arrow! *Here.*' He jabbed his hip. 'Damn cow went bloody bonkers, rampaging through the—oh, I'm sorry.' He turned to Marcus. 'Caught up in the excitement, I completely forgot my manners. I'm Cassius Gallus, importer of fine Parian marble.' He held out his hand. Orbilio shook it. 'And you are?'

'Trying to find the joker who shot it.'

· · · ·

THERE MUST BE A DOZEN reasons why someone would choose to fire an arrow at a sacrificial bull outside Jupiter's temple on New Year's Day, but for the life of her, Claudia couldn't think of one. On the other hand, the reasons why someone would want to take a pot shot at a politician could fill a book, and then some.

'Don't look at me,' she said. 'I don't have the strength to draw a bow, I have an alibi, and there's no way I'd waste money ordering a hit on some slimy official before he's even taken office—assuming I knew, or even cared, who this year's consuls are.'

Or indeed had the money to begin with.

'Strangely,' Orbilio rumbled, 'I didn't have you pegged as the Amazon Queen.'

'Oh, I don't know,' Cassius said. 'I can just picture you as Diana of the Hunt, darling. All those cute, cuddly, little furry creatures at your feet.'

Bang on cue, Claudia's dark Egyptian cat bounded in from the garden, and immediately started hissing and yowling at the intrusion of strangers, advancing sideways, back arched, while trying to decide whose face to claw off first. It was tough to tell which way the verdict was headed, given that Drusilla was cross-eyed, but Cassius obviously felt that bridegrooms need all the available face space they can get on their wedding day. Whereas a scar or six can only enhance a Security Policeman's aspect.

'Excuuuuuse me while I check the slaves have laid out your New Year presents properly.'

Orbilio watched him go. 'You aren't seriously marrying that prat? He walks like he's got salt in his loin cloth, his IQ's lower than the temperature outside, dammit he'd be out of his depth in a puddle.'

Anyone else with those narrowed eyes and clenched fists, and you'd think they were jealous.

'As opposed to Marcus Cornelius Orbilio, who sets low standards and consistently fails to meet them?'

'Ha-ha-very-funny.'

'I thought so.' She moved closer to the brazier. 'Now, if you're not here to throw me in irons for conspiring to bring down the Empire, do you mind telling me the point of your visit?'

'Suppose I said I came to talk you out of marrying him?'

'Of course you did. Someone tries to assassinate one of the two second highest-ranking officials in the Empire and you have no idea which one, while the sacrificial bull stampedes through the crowd, injuring goodness knows how many spectators—'

'One dead, fourteen injured, it's a miracle there weren't more casualties.'

'—why wouldn't you take time off to give me a spot of relationship advice?'

'For gods' sakes, Claudia, he was caught *in flagrante* the night you announced your engagement.'

'I know. I was there.' It was her own damn house, for pity's sake. 'But Cassius isn't used to heavy drinking. After a few too many, he blacked out, that little kitchen slut seduced him—'

'Whoa. You're telling me he's out cold, and she ... what? helps herself?'

'What I'm telling you is that Cassius is as honest as the day is long, and what he lacks in brains, he more than makes up for in integrity. I believe him, I do, when he said he couldn't remember one damn thing about it. And that if—*if*—anything happened, which by the way he doubted, he must have assumed she was me, and...well, reacted accordingly.'

'I still think you're making a mistake.'

She watched the only patrician member of the Security Police pace the gleaming marble flooring of her office like a panther. Funny, really. The price of the Attican wool that went into his toga would feed a family in the slums for six months, while the gold ring on his finger would keep them for the remainder of the year. And that's the thing. The aristocracy flirt with the lower classes, they'll happily eat and drink with them, even sleep with them. But they'd lose their status, their inheritance, and their families would disown them if they took it further, so they sure as hell don't commit. Especially when they're relentlessly ambitious.

'I may have my faults, Marcus, but being wrong isn't one of them. So why don't you stop teasing my cat, and go solve a bullicide or something.'

'Ah. Well. That's where it gets complicated.'

He pulled up a high-backed chair upholstered in iridescent damask with legs carved into lions' paws, sat down by the brazier and crossed his feet at the ankles. Sensing permanency, not to mention a boot that looked as if it contained a fair old kick, Drusilla snaked out into the peristyle to wreak vengeance on the mice.

'Since it's virtually impossible to kill a bull with just a single arrow, the general consensus is that the intended target was one of the newly elected consuls.'

'But?'

'When each consul is surrounded by twelve armed bodyguards—' freedmen exempt from military duty, who also held annual appointments '—not to mention hordes of acolytes, assistants, augurs and the haruspex, we have a problem.'

'What about the Priest of Jupiter?'

We, you notice. The sneaky bastard said *we* have a problem.

The hell *we* do.

'Top job,' she said. 'New to it. Maybe one of the others on the shortlist felt they were better equipped? And what about that long list of taboos and restrictions that come with it? Suppose he ate something containing flour or beans by mistake, and the person whose house where he dined felt they'd been cursed? Or he accidentally touched iron, the person holding it later died, and the family wanted revenge? The arrow could just as easily have had the priest's name on it.'

'I'm with you on that first point. Either of the others on the shortlist would have made a better fist of it, but that man's so crooked, he could hide behind a spiral staircase. Word is, he bought the vote, but that doesn't change things.' Marcus sucked his teeth. 'Either the archer has an exceptionally good eye, and can take a target out with just a single shot—

'—or he lets loose a full quiver, to be sure.'

'Exactly. Neither of those things happened, and while I can't rule out the possibility that someone nudged his elbow at the last knockings, or he tripped and lost his footing as he fired, *or* smoke blew in his eyes, *or* he just happened to sneeze at the wrong moment, the chances of any of that happening are thinner than a beggar's cloak in winter.'

She sighed. 'Square one, it seems.'

'Pretty sure I saw the sign pinned to your door when I came in, saying *welcome back.*'

'Welcome back?' Cassius breezed. 'Very nice of you, but I hadn't actually left. I only went to check on my lovely fiancée's presents—um...'

He scanned the room for crossed blue eyes. Simultaneously, Claudia and Marcus pointed to the dark space beneath the lowest library shelf.

'...and I haven't finished yet. Ta-ta!'

Dammit, if that Security Policeman thought Claudia had any intention of meeting the snigger in his eyes, he could bloody well think again.

• • • •

FOREIGN AMBASSADORS left the city with the firm impression that Roman revels ran from the middle of December right through until the middle of January without a break, and in many respects they weren't wrong. All the hard work that went into collecting, weaving, and putting up those swags and swathes and wreaths and garlands for Saturnalia? Who in their right mind's going to take them down, only to put the wretched things back up in seven days? If the greenery started to wilt, then maybe it was changed. But oily leaves cling hard to life. A month of decorated windows, doors and stairs it was!

Besides. After a summer of hard fighting, dusty milling work or slogging on the farms, citizens and slaves alike deserved a break, and it wasn't as if there were any pressing demands on their workload. The seas had closed and where, a few short weeks ago, the wharves rang with the clatter of ladders and carts, trolleys and barrows, shouts, hammers and braying, the only sound now was the creak of ungreased pulleys and the crying of gulls. Out in the fields, ploughing or sowing wasn't permitted until the auspices were pronounced on the Ides, confining agricultural activities to the dull routine of sharpening stakes, clearing out ditches and the occasional bit of pruning. And since the campaigning season didn't kick off for another couple of months, what better opportunity for a soldier with time on his hands to nab a hare with the slingshot, or fix all those fiddly odd jobs round the house?

Yessir. Ten days of feasting in the middle did no one any harm. Quite the opposite, in fact. And as Orbilio's long stride ate up the slope of the Capitoline Rise, he reflected on how there was a time when a consul's authority was formidable and extensive. Even when he was growing up, at least one of the pair had to be forty-three years old, and back then (all of thirty years ago!) both had to have served a prior praetorship—experience they'd needed in spades, if they were to be entrusted with the management of wars. But a combination of peace and the expansion of Rome's boundaries gave the provinces more and more autonomy, and slowly, the role of the consuls became downgraded. They still presided over the Senate, and they were still in charge of managing the Games (which were still funded out of their own pockets, some things never change!) These days, however, age and experience were irrelevant, and even the consulship itself had become a transitory office, with the holders stepping down every few months, to make room for fresh blood.

Having said that, the New Year's inauguration remained a momentous occasion. The bestowing of an honour that ensured the consuls were remembered for posterity, since the year—their official term of office—would be named after them.

'You were right about the arrow's trajectory, sir.' A youth in uniform, barely old enough to shave, saluted. 'It was fired from the roof of the Temple of Plenty opposite. The rope's still there.'

'Don't tell me.' Marcus returned the salute. 'Several people saw him throw the grappling hook, they all believed it was some show-off, wanting a bird's eye view of the proceedings, but no one physically saw him shoot.'

The soldier shrugged. 'All eyes were on the procession.'

They would be. Horns were blowing. There was music. Incense. The bull, decked in garlands and sacred sash, was being led to the altar, ready to be stunned before its throat was slit. The archer would have hidden the bow inside his heavy winter cloak to shin up the rope. Calculated that one arrow was all he could fire off in the time available. Before sliding back down and melting into the chaos.

'I have a description, though.'

'Let me guess. Young, swarthy, dark hair worn longer than usual?'

The soldier's jaw dropped. 'How did you know? Especially the bit about the hair?'

'That level of marksmanship suggests our shooter is a Cretan.'

The best light missile troops in the business.

'Then he shouldn't be too hard to round up. There's a small Cretan community near the Harbour Gate, another along the Appian Way—'

Orbilio didn't pop the new recruit's bubble, and in any case it was important every lead was followed, considering the consuls and the priest were three of the most powerful and influential citizens in Rome. But he knew, before they started, the exercise was a waste of time. Not because tight communities don't rat one another out, but because Cretans were foreigners, and therefore subject to torture. Nightingales don't sing sweeter, once the pliers are flexed. Personally, Marcus felt honey trapped more flies than spikes or hot metal, but in this case, the archer was undoubtedly on a horse halfway to Anywhere-But-Here. Today's events had been carefully planned and immaculately orchestrated. Nothing would be left to chance, especially arresting an archer who would quickly reveal the name of the man who hired him, in exchange for immunity from the heinous crime of scratching a bull's backside.

The question, right from the beginning, had been "why".

Find the motive, close the case, and that's the reason Orbilio dropped in on Claudia this morning. To bounce ideas around.

Oh, yes.

And talk her out of marriage to that prat.

• • • •

CLAUDIA HAD NO INTENTION of being talked out of anything, especially marriage to that prat. She wasn't looking for a soul mate, and in any case, she didn't have the luxury of waiting for Mister Right to swan her way.

The law was unequivocal. A widow must re-marry within two years of her husband's demise, and if she didn't choose the groom herself, then the State would step in and assign one.

Bugger that.

So while Cassius might not be the intellectual catch of the century, he was easy on the eye, honest to a T, and rich beyond Claudia's wildest dreams. Better still, he was acquainted, not to mention sympathetic, to the tragic circumstances two years earlier, when, on the very point of re-marriage, Claudia's future husband dropped dead of natural causes.

'Four years a widow. Why, you poor old lonely darling.'

'Not so much of the old, if you don't mind.'

See? He laughed at her jokes, too. No, no, she thought, watching Cassius strolling round the peristyle, ducking moths that hadn't hibernated due to the exceptionally mild winter, but suddenly wishing they had, as they sizzled in the flames of thousands of fragrant oil lamps set up round the topiaries and statues. Cassius was perfect.

Must be the lighting, because for a split second his face merged with that of a tall, witty, policeman with a baritone voice, who smelled of sandalwood, with a faint hint of the rosemary in which his tunic had been rinsed.

'Ninety nine percent of Rome's citizens are decent, honest, hardworking folk,' she'd quipped, before Marcus left for the Capitol. 'It's that other one percent that lets the side down, but that's the fault of you patricians for electing them.'

'Careful,' he'd warned with a grin. 'I'm not in the Senate yet.'

Yet. Notice that? If proof was needed that the lines between plebs and patricians remained clearly drawn, look no further. Urbanity was a cover, and the moral of the story?

Never trust a man who smells of sandalwood.

So she'd quickly moved the conversation on, suggesting what he'd no doubt worked out for himself.

That the intended target was the bull.

• • • •

ORBILIO HAD INDEED come to that conclusion, even before half a dozen men rushed forward and stunned it in its tracks, then slaughtered it before it inflicted further damage. In less than the blink of his professional eye, he'd assessed the crush of religious and political officials clustered in front of the temple, and an even larger crowd than usual, thanks to the unseasonal clement weather, and concluded that not even the sharpest marksman could pick out a target from that lot.

Then miss with such spectacular success.

So why the bull?

'A crack shot with a massive white lump of beef in his sights?' Claudia's reasoning had followed his own lines of deduction. 'The objective wasn't to kill it.'

Had the arrow lodged in its neck, that might be different. In theory, Cretan archers wouldn't give a stuff about unleashing the wrath of a god they didn't believe in on a people who'd subjugated their island. In practice, however, Cretans worshipped Zeus, who happened to share startlingly similar characteristics to Jupiter, not least being King of the Gods. And while neither Claudia or Marcus could say whether bulls were still sacred on Crete, Orbilio was willing to bet a year's salary that no mercenary, however well paid, would risk slaying one.

Also, when it comes to public sacrifice, the bull is the only animal that isn't asked permission and forgiveness. In other words, the only creature that doesn't lay down its life willingly, but is cowed into submission, pun intended.

A lone arrow, flying from the Temple of Plenty and killing it outright, would have been the best portent imaginable.

'Shall I tell you what I think?' he'd asked, rocking on his toes with his back to the brazier.

'It if stops you warming your brains in favour of arresting bull molesters, I'm all ears.'

'It does.'

'Then the faster you talk, the better.'

He was definitely making headway, he thought happily. In the past, she'd accused his brains of being set equally low on his anatomy, but at the front, rather than the rear.

'I think the whole idea was to wreck the auspices for the consuls' inauguration.'

But this is where Marcus Cornelius Orbilio came unstuck.

There wasn't a single person who would benefit from it.

• • • •

JUGGLERS, ACROBATS, fire eaters, you couldn't ask for more. Pan-pipes livened up the action, a Greek harpist calmed things down, a thin young man dressed as an Etruscan king sang poetry, as he strummed his lyre of gleaming tortoiseshell.

'This is magnificent, darling. Truly outstanding.' Cassius' dark eyes shone with admiration, pride, and perhaps a little too much wine. 'Black drapes across the left side of the ceiling, as Janus looks to the past, white on the right, as he looks to the future. I had no idea you had such an artistic eye—oh, Claudia, we'll throw such wonderful banquets when we're married, won't we?'

'Two a week, three in the summer.'

'At least! And where on earth did you find such a brilliant puppeteer? He must have cost a fortune!'

'These things always come with strings attached.'

'You're so funny. And beautiful. I love the way you feed me oysters and flamingo tongues with your fingers, and the way your hair bounces and your hips sway when you walk.' He leaned closer. 'You know, I could eat you right now.'

'In front of two senators, three magistrates and a judge? Here.'

She dipped a chunk of chestnut bread in her bowl of hot, spiced wine sauce and fed it to him. Cassius all but purred. And while those same senators, magistrates and judges feasted on dormice in honey and sweet sucking pig with their glamorous wives, the wine flowed, the music played, and dancers dressed as wood nymphs and water nymphs wove in and out of the couches, swaying with sensual rhythm to the click of castanets and the soft rustle of tambourines.

'And now, my friends—'

At the roll of drums, Claudia stood up. The dining hall fell silent.

'—in honour of the great god, Janus, who will bring us good fortune throughout the coming year—'

Another dramatic drum roll.

'—I give you the star of tonight's banquet... *CAPRICORN!*'

Capricorn, of course, was the current astrology sign, and the sign under which the Emperor Augustus himself, the blessed Octavian, had been born, and all power to her cook, he'd come up with a stunning creation of the fish/goat hybrid. Mainly goat, of course. Basted with spices and spit roasted, but with a fish tail made of bread that had been baked so the "scales" were the same colour as the body.

'Hurrah!'

'Bravo!'

Claudia accepted the accolades with becoming modesty, then turned to her future groom, to invite him, as guest of honour, to carve.

'Cassius?'

The space beside her on the couch was empty.

In the corner, there was a flurry of activity among the slaves. Leonides moved forward, whispered in her ear, but too late. Scandal, travelling faster than the speed of light, had already spread her cloak over the banquet. Before Claudia's horrified hand shot to her mouth, two senators, three magistrates and a judge, not to mention their glamorous wives, had rushed to an alcove screened off from the dining hall. Where, sprawled over the cushions, was Cassius Gallus, passed out with a smile on his face.

On his left, a water nymph was rushing to cover her modesty with a wisp of blue cotton.

On his right, a wood nymph, wearing nothing but a pretty green garland and Cassius's hand on her breast, promptly burst into tears.

• • • •

'WHEN YOU SAID THERE wasn't room for me on your seating plan,' a baritone rumbled, 'I'd rather assumed it was because the banquet was full. Not because no one was invited.'

An hour had passed, in which a marriage was cancelled, a flurry of embarrassed guests packed up and left, entertainers were dismissed, the staff given the night off, and Claudia's blue-eyed, cross-eyed dark Egyptian cat had decided that abandoned titbits in the warmth were infinitely preferable to abandoned mouseholes in the cold.

'Funny.' Claudia surveyed the mountains of congealing quails, lobsters and sucking pig, watched over by both of Janus's bearded faces. 'I thought you'd be busy delivering reports, rising through the ranks, and whatever else it is you security chappies do when they're not teasing peoples' cats.'

'Yes, about that. Shall we talk in your office?'

Poor Drusilla. Just when she had a nice, juicy ankle in her sights, too.

'I came to tell you that you were a hundred percent spot on,' he said, leaning back in the chair, feet propped on her desk, ankles safely out of the way. 'The bull was a distraction.'

He couldn't understand who'd benefit from a year's bad luck—

'Unless it has nothing to do with consuls, priests or sacrifice,' Claudia had said, 'and everything to do with murder.'

Only one person died when the bull went berserk, she pointed out.

'If I were you, I'd see what they actually died of.'

Stab wound to the heart, as it happened. A praetor with more money than sense discovered that his wife had taken a lover, then hired himself a marksman, knowing that, outside the temple, the bull would be quickly subdued before it could inflict too much harm. The instant the arrow hit, he killed his rival and pushed him under the rampaging animal.

'The perfect murder, if it hadn't been for you.'

Claudia fixed her gaze on the statue of Janus, centre stage in the office, looking to the past and to the future.

'It's not easy being right, Orbilio, but someone has to do it. Drink to toast the New Year?'

'Wine, please—just not the stuff you gave Cassius.'

'Seriously? My bridegroom's caught cheating with not just one floozy, but two—' can't talk your way out of that, can you? can't pretend you thought both of them were me? '—in the middle of my banquet, and if that isn't humiliation enough, you accuse me of tampering with his wine!'

She sank the contents of Cassius's goblet, along with the rest of the flagon.

'There's nothing wrong with the damned wine.'

Why do you think I fed him those morsels by hand? And for gods' sake, it wasn't *salt* in his loin cloth. More an interesting little blend of Eastern herbs, that left him in a permanent state of arousal.

'So it's coincidence that you have another two years of freedom, before you need to find a husband?'

'What else?'

Quite frankly, however much she'd slipped that hired "kitchen slut" and those two dancing girls, Claudia would have willingly paid them double.

Happy New Year, everyone!

FOOL'S GOLD

'**P**lease,' I said. 'Would one of you mind telling me what a yewcan is?'

Heiresses, you should know, have two traits in common. One is that, knock-kneed or plump, silly or smart, they are curiously popular. Men, always men, hang on their every word. Which is why I knew Mr. Stanmore, head of Stanmore, Sutherland & Reid, Solicitors, and the gentleman who handled my father's vast estate, would not ignore me the way he would, for instance, his own wife. Neither would Mr. Pettigrew, the dashing young blade so desperate to become my husband and who assured me, perhaps a few too many times, that it was pure coincidence he was Mr. Stanmore's nephew, our introduction being nothing more than a felicitous twist of fate. Although he did have the grace to regret it took place at my father's funeral.

'Miss Merrick?' queried Mr. Stanmore over the top of his pince-nez, and was that another new suit of clothes he was wearing? With another brand new watch chain gleaming on that expensive, tailored waistcoat?

'A yewcan,' I prompted. 'Only you and Mr. Pettigrew have been discussing it for some time—' in my drawing room, facing my terrace, overlooking my extensive parklands and in such a way that the conversation was designed to fly right over my not-so-pretty little head '—and I am curious to understand why such an item might be so popular, and why so many men are rushing to acquire one.'

Below his luxuriously barbered moustache, Mr. Stanmore smiled at me the way I imagined he would smile at a small lap dog, a Pomeranian, for instance, and all but petted me. 'Not yew-can, Miss Merrick. We are discussing the Yukon in Canada, where gold was recently discovered in the Klondike River.'

'Vast quantities of gold.' Mr. Pettigrew elaborated, shifting forward in his chair. Well, my chair to be precise. Sumptuously upholstered in velvet, royal purple I think they call it, with gilded arms and carved legs, he seemed very much at home in the thing. One might even say, a little too much at home.

'Dear me.' I fluffed my leg o'mutton sleeves. 'As if there isn't enough jewellery in the world already.'

119

'Gold will save the world, Miss Merrick,' he said, with a glint in his eye that rivalled his uncle's watch chain. 'Just as the rush to find it will also change the world.'

I intended to let out that endearing non-committal squeak I keep rehearsing in the mirror, but in practice I do believe I grunted, because he went on to explain how a series of financial shocks had undermined public confidence in North America, leading to financial panic which in turn resulted in a deep, and countrywide, depression.

'Gripped by the same changes sweeping Great Britain, the United States have seen their farm-based societies overtaken by rampant industrializaton, Miss Merrick, their cities flooded with workers and with people looking for work, which was fine. Until the Depression set in.'

Fine, I supposed, if you don't mind smoke corroding your lungs, having your pockets picked by vagabonds and thieves, your throat slit for the last sixpence you own, and are content to send your children up the chimneys, to the factories, down the coal mines.

'It is your belief that finding gold in the Klondike River will miraculously reverse this situation?'

'I don't believe in miracles, Miss Merrick. What I do believe is that hard work pays off.' Mr. Pettigrew shifted closer, the glint in his eye stronger than ever. 'Every banknote that is printed in America has to be backed by the equivalent amount in gold held in reserve.'

This was known as the gold standard, he explained, and at the height—or was it nadir—of the Panic, certain people began propounding that the scarcity of gold would limit the number of banknotes in circulation, and have an even more harmful effect on an already depressed economy.

One of my accomplishments lies in the gentle art of encouraging nods, and while Mr. Pettigrew expounded on the report in the happy belief that he had my full attention, I had, in fact, turned at least half of it on his uncle.

I know Stanmore is skimming. He has been for some time. The problem is, I am quite unable to prove it. In the wake of my father's death (was it really four years ago?), he brought in the keenest accountants and the shrewdest firm of stockbrokers one could hope to engage. Who are doubtless swindling me, as well. Heaven knows, there is enough to go round.

'It is estimated that already one hundred thousand prospectors have tried to find their fortunes in that river.'

'A hundred thousand,' I murmured. 'My, my.'

Greed, I find, to be the worst of the seven deadly sins, don't you? The worst possible commandment to break, too.

Even above thou shalt not kill.

• • • •

OH, AND THE OTHER TRAIT we heiresses share is distrust. Dense, pressing, cloying and dark, with roots deeper than the tallest oak, it is every bit a part of us as our green eyes, bony ankles and red hair that will not, and I mean will not, be tamed. And just like the freckles on our skin, every ugly inch, suspicion cannot be eradicated.

• • • •

MR. PETTIGREW IS NOT unattractive. He is lean without running to sinew and bone, has blue eyes that seem startlingly out of place beneath that coronet of long black hair, and a jaw that puts most lanterns to shame. More than once I have allowed his hand to accidentally brush mine, occasionally my shoulder, for no other reason than I enjoy the sensation it engenders. Enjoy it very much. You see, the simple truth of the matter is (and why I have not dismissed him the way of other suitors) because marriage, I am told, entails lengthy and vigorous duties in the bedroom. Now while no heiress is ever past marriageable age and, heaven knows I have held out longer than most, I want children. Lots of children. I want girls, I want boys, I want twins, I want dogs, I want cats and guinea pigs and hamsters and rabbits. In short, I want love.

Love is not a commodity in which I have had much trade in my twenty-three years. My sister died of whooping cough when I was six and she was four, a tragedy my father marked by instantly siring a replacement, and although my mother worshipped me—*ah, Caroline, my little Red Riding Head*—she died precisely nine months later, giving birth to a stillborn child. From that point on, my father immersed himself in the business of the coal mines that so generously funded this vast Gloucestershire park and neo-Classical mansion, and if I saw him twice a year, I counted myself lucky.

Who imagined a princess in a palace would have so much in common with an orphan in the workhouse?

Love, of course, is not something Mr. Pettigrew will bring to the marriage, should I accept his proposal. But if he can be the instrument, and a pleasurable one at that, to bring the love I so desperately crave into my life, I would be a fool to let such an opportunity pass me by.

It will not come again.

• • • •

IT IS RARE THAT I SEE Mr. Pettigrew more than once a week. He will escort me to the theatre, or perhaps dinner with a bunch of frightful bores, where we will discuss Society and the weather, but never, ever anything of a personal nature or offer an opinion that might give us an insight into one another's soul. I do not wish to know how thieves operate, much less the workings of a mind that is hell-bent on sucking me dry. Like the miners in the Yukon, who light fires to thaw the permafrost until it becomes soft enough to dig, then light another, then another, then another, he would have to work hard to find out what makes me tick. And, to use another parallel, he was unlikely to strike gold there, as well.

Some Sunday afternoons we might promenade in the park like the loving couple we are supposed to be, him in his brushed Derby and striped trousers, me in my big hat with big feathers and corset in which I can barely breathe. Heads turn. People stop to admire us. At least, that is what Mr. Pettigrew insists. I suspect, if they admire anything, it is the quality of my silk, though more likely they are deafened by its rustle, shocked that so many plumes can fit on one small head, and puzzled as to how many species are still not yet extinct in the name of female fashion.

Personally, however, I do not believe they stare in admiration. Disdain, more like, that such a handsome specimen would stoop so low to snag a red-headed spinster long past marriageable age. Resentment, too, perhaps, that that spinster has more money than she can spend in twenty lifetimes. But if I had to bet my enormous coal-brought fortune, I would wager it was out of pity that they stopped. Because without aforesaid inheritance, aforesaid spinster would be lucky to have bagged a balding baker.

The point being, it was out of character for Mr. Pettigrew to roll up unannounced on a Thursday morning. Especially when I had only just had an audience with him and his uncle the afternoon before.

'Please,' I was about to say, 'take a seat,' but he had already thrown himself into a mahogony Chippendale chair as though he had twenty at home, all equally intricately carved, with cabriole legs and lion's paw feet, and who knows? Maybe he was skimming those off me, too. Sneaking them out, one chair at a time.

'I can't stop thinking about the Gold Rush.' He didn't give me chance to tell him what I might have been thinking. 'You remember my uncle explained how it started? Three men hitting pay dirt in Rabbit Creek?'

'Now renamed Bonanza Creek for somewhat obvious reasons? I do remember.'

'How tramdrivers are abandoning their trolleys, firemen are abandoning their trucks, even policemen are abandoning their stations to join the search for riches?'

'Farms sold at knock-down prices, homes mortgaged, loans taken out that will have crippling and devastating consequences, simply in order to kit out the stampeders with the most basic of needs? Stove, tools, a ton of supplies?'

And I do mean a ton. Quite literally. The Canadian Government insisted on them taking a year's worth of provisions into the mountains with them. Oats, beans, flour, matches. Buckets, axes, blankets, canvas. Entering the Territory was risk enough, they reasoned. A foolish man might freeze to death, but no man would starve out there. Not if they could help it.

'Never mind the exorbitant costs of reaching such a remote area,' I added.

Packages were available for those able to afford the $27,000 (yes thousand) fare, the rich man's route they call it, taking stampeders from Seattle to the delta via steamship, then ferrying them sixteen hundred miles upriver. But even those who made the journey overland were obliged to pay guides who, for an eye-watering fee, would pilot them through boat-splintering rapids. Then be forced to negotiate with unscrupulous sorts charging unscrupulous tolls to cross "their" makeshift bridge over a mudhole. Heavens, even pack animals commanded unimaginable prices, never mind they were, for the most part, worn-out nags unfit for such journeys. Indeed, one route has been named "Dead Horse Trail" for that very reason. No match for the boulder fields, bogs and sharp rocks, these frail creatures dropped like flies, littering the track with their rotting corpses, and in such profusion it was impossible to remove them. In the end, their bodies were simply ground down by the endless procession of feet and hooves.

All in the pursuit of a few lumps of metal.

'Strange,' Mr. Pettigew murmured. 'I do not recall discussing loans or supplies yesterday. Much less the challenges of travel. Although, interestingly, that does bring me round to what I wished to say.'

His hands, I noticed, were clasped together, the knuckles white. His blue eyes shone.

'It is already established, Miss Merrick, that a combination of the harshness of the Yukon climate and the trials of negotiating the few, and extremely treacherous, routes up to the Klondike, has eliminated more than two-thirds of the hundred thousand who set out.'

Not all the stampeders met the same fate as their horses, although too many poor souls have. Husbands, fathers, brothers, sons, falling victim to the marrow-biting cold, or infected wounds that never healed. Some died from falling off the slippery, narrow paths that skirt the gorges and ravines, or disease triggered by mosquito-ridden swamps. And more than a few, I'm afraid, drowned when the fleet of hopelessly unseaworthy vessels capsized, their captains hoping to make a fortune from transporting the prospectors, but whose avarice turned their overloaded, overcrowded boats into lonely, floating coffins.

But the vast majority who set off for the Yukon simply couldn't cope with taking three months, and forty trips up and down the mountain, just to ferry their provisions across one single pass. Or sitting out the winter in tents beside the frozen lakes. A hundred miles of frozen lakes. Some were driven mad by perpetual darkness, others by perpetual sunlight, yet more by the clouds of flies and almost constant feuds and squabbles. Accepting they were out of their depth, they turned back. Penniless and broken men.

'It is my opinion, Miss Merrick, that, of the small percentage who make it through, only a fraction will strike it rich.'

I was inclined to agree.

'Isolation will grind even the toughest man down,' I replied. Spring had come to Gloucestershire practically overnight. Like Chinese lanterns, the willows lining the river dangled brilliant, lime-green fronds in the gently flowing water. Daffodils turned their heads towards the house like periscopes. 'Those lucky ones who do find gold will probably drink or gamble it away during the long, dark winter months, just to pass away the time.'

'More likely, after eight months of bacon and canned beans, they will gladly trade their riches for the excitement of fresh eggs and peaches, paper, pen and ink.'

I looked up a little more sharply than intended. I had not taken Mr. Pettigrew for a man of such perception.

'Many more,' he continued, 'will swap their finds for different kinds of nuggets, reasoning that news from home is far more valuable.'

'It being your opinion that it will be the purveyors of news and eggs, of mosquito nets and tent poles, in short the people who provide home comforts in the form of apple pies baked in hammered-out tin cans, who are the men and women who will really strike it rich?'

I opened the French doors to the terrace and indicated that we might take a stroll outside. The late March sun was warm, swelling the buds on the horse chestnuts in the most satisfying manner, and had already melted the frost that twinkled on the path when I awoke at dawn.

'Wealth is relative,' he said, offering his arm. 'When I said yesterday that Klondike gold would change the world, I meant in terms of the change it would bring to everyone, not just the stampeders, their guides, and those who kit them out.'

I slipped my arm in his and moved closer to his body, on the pretext that the tickling breeze was far colder than it was. In doing so, I caught the smell of oil of bay tinged with cinnamon, and while the notion of being addressed as Mrs. Pettigrew held no appeal (Pettigrew! I ask you!), it occurred to me that I ought not delay much longer in accepting his proposal.

'Towns are already rising and thriving from the Gold Rush,' I agreed. 'Many have hotels, theatres, churches and schools.'

'One already has the reputation of being the Paris of the North.'

'Your point yesterday being that gold will put paid to America's Depression.' I liked the feel of his strong arm linked with mine. 'For one thing, it will bring railways.'

'Roads.'

'The motor car industry is set to explode, now that Mr. Ford and Mr. Peugeot have ironed out the creases, and every rich man in the industrialized world feels the need to own one.'

'If the United States *do* buy out the French, work will recommence sooner rather than later on the Panama Ship Canal, bringing destinations even closer.'

'Some Norwegian, I believe his name is Amundsen, is convinced he can succeed where others failed, and navigate a passage to the Pacific Northwest via the Arctic Ocean.' I looked up at the blossoms on the cherry tree. Beautiful, long-awaited, but fleeting. 'You're going, aren't you?'

He stopped. Turned. Looked down at me with what looked like pain in his eyes. With a jolt, I realized, far too late, this was what passion looked like.

'A new century dawns, Miss Merrick, and with it comes industry, jobs, prosperity and success. Sue me for breach of promise, if you will—'

'That would be somewhat difficult, since I have not accepted your proposal.'

'Then understand why I need to be part of this new and exciting world.'

'I do, Mr. Pettigrew.' I swallowed. 'I understand very much, but tell me.' Another fluff of the sleeves, another tweak of the gown and my, my, doesn't silk compose a pretty melody? 'Is it your intendion to become one of those purveyors of fruit, eggs and news? A seller of heavy undergarments, perhaps? A saloon keeper? A supplier of greatcoats, picks and shovels? A—'

'Photographer.'

'*Photographer?*' It is, I was taught in finishing school, quite unladylike to goggle. But goggle I most assuredly did. 'Where on earth will you find the equipment?'

'I already have the equipment.'

Aha. The Chippendale chairs.

'But-but-but...' My head was reeling. 'How can you possibly learn such a complex trade at short notice?'

Would I be able to trace the stolen goods (when did I last check the family silver?) through sale at an auction house? At long last find the proof I so desperately need, that he and his uncle have been robbing me blind?

While losing my last chance of gaining the love I so desperately crave...

'Miss Merrick.' He almost smiled. 'If you had once asked what I did for a living, enquired just *once* how I passed my days, you would know that I am a photographer by profession.' He paused. 'Unfortunately, Society portraits and weddings, no matter how lucrative, are no match for images of old-timers digging through the permafrost. Of men facing raging snowstorms, frozen rivers and mountainous terrain in their lust for glory. Or,' he grinned, 'saloon girls kicking up the can-can in a line across the street.'

The way he spoke, I couldn't just picture them. I could almost hear them, smell them, touch them.

'I want to show this changing world the hardships and the pain, the tragedies and the triumphs, those apple pies you talked about, baked in hammered-out tin cans. I want the public to look into the eyes of the clairvoyants who happily take money from desperate individuals in exchange for telling them where to dig for non-existent seams of gold.'

'You need to capture, too, the native tribes, Mr. Pettigrew, before our white-man snobbery and our white-man diseases wipe them out completely, and before their hunting grounds and legends disappear.'

At last, a real smile. One that dimpled his cheeks and softened his eyes. 'Please, Miss Merrick! There is only so much that once man can achieve!'

'I know.' I smiled back. 'Which is exactly why I'm coming with you.'

* * * *

'W-WHAT HAPPENED?'

Mr. Pettigrew was lying on my bed, in my house, with my feather pillows propping his head, for the simple reason that I have no relatives, no real friends, certainly no acquaintances I would wish to invite under my roof, and this was the only bed made. Dr. Proctor (a name even sillier than Pettigrew) was standing over him, stethoscope taking soundings between ears and chest, so I answered for him.

'It appears that not all the frost on the path had melted.'

As he spun round at my announcement, he slipped. Cracked his head on the path.

'Lucky for you, young man, the back of the skull is where the bone is the thickest.' Dr Proctor (forgive my sniggering again) forced a glass of something green and treacly down Mr. Pettigrew's throat, and even though he was barely conscious, I didn't blame him using his last burst of energy on a grimace.

'C-c-c-' he said faintly, beckoning me forward.

I held my breath, my heart beating just that little bit faster, waiting for him to whisper my name. Caroline.

'C-c-cognac,' he said.

. . . .

'WHAT IS THAT?'

Several hours had passed, in which he had slept, so my maid told me, like a baby, and which I had spent on the telephone – such a wonderful invention! – booking two passages from Liverpool to the Yukon, via Cape Town, San Francisco and Seattle. First class should at least take the edge off, although for the cost of the tickets, I believe I could have paid for completion of the work on the Panama Ship Canal singlehandedly. And cut a great deal of time off the voyage in the process.

'Cognac,' I said.

'Thank you, that is most kind, but-' he struggled to sit up, 'I can't stand the stuff.'

'That's what knocks to the head do.' I heaved him forward, fluffed his (my!) pillows, and wondered why a touch of stubble on the jaw should be so socially unacceptable. 'Make you ask for things you don't want.'

What I would do when we arrived in the Yukon, I hadn't the foggiest idea. But to live a life of emptiness, however luxurious, knowing it was built on the lives of men, women and children who'd heaved and hammered at a coal face hundreds of feet below the ground, day in, day out, until it killed them, was no life at all.

'I don't care if your uncle is creaming my inheritance,' I said. 'And I don't care if you only want—'

'Why would my uncle do that?' Mr. Pettigrew frowned. 'He owns stakes in the Hudson's Bay Company that not only ferries stampeders to Alaska for $27,000 a pop, he is also an investor in other steamship companies engaged in the same business.'

In my shock, I almost forgot how most of the prospectors, who used their entire life savings on a water route to save valuable time, were city slickers who had no idea how to survive in gruelling conditions. Too often, that $27,000 was a one-way ticket in more ways than one.

'Mr. Stanmore's rich?'

'Wealthier than you, Miss Merrick. Which is why the Yukon is so important to him, and why it invades almost every conversation in which he is involved.'

'But he's a solicitor!'

'Whose brother happens to be a stockbroker, which is how he became involved.' He looked sideways at me. 'You do know you're his only client?'

'I am?' Unladylike to goggle, unladylike to squeak.

'He is very fond of you-'

'You mean, he feels sorry for me.'

'That, too. But he did not feel it appropriate to leave you high and dry until you were, um...married.'

'Which is why he made you tag along?'

'He made me tag along for the simple reason that, not to put too fine a point on it, he is scared stiff of you, Miss Merrick. Like me, he is well aware you are not the fluffy little thing you would have him believe, that you deliberately mislead him into thinking you are unread and unintelligent, and he found it most unnerving. Of course, now we know why. You mistrusted him. But your duplicity is the reason he insisted I join him at your father's funeral. Moral support.'

'But...if he's rich, and you're a man of independent means, why did you ask me to marry you?'

'Why do you think?' he laughed, pulling me down on the pillows. 'And just to be clear, I wasn't delusional, calling for cognac. I was indeed calling for you, Mrs. Pettigrew. You, and your luscious cognac curls.'

I'm sure, over time, the name will grow on me.

LONG SLOW DANCE THROUGH
THE PASSAGE OF TIME

A n owl hoots from the ancient, spreading oak. Voles rustle through the fallen leaves along the hedgerow. The bell of St. Giles tolls three.

Lying here in the dark, my thoughts turn to Richard.

Then again.

My thoughts always turn to Richard.

• • • •

'MISS SNEED, WHAT A pleasure. I've heard so much about you.'

Perhaps I looked at him too sharply, 'cause he blushed.

'Nothing bad, you understand. Quite the contrary. It's just that my parishioners...well, some of them gossip...oh, not in a spiteful way. I meant the way they chatter...'

Funny how people stammer and gush to cover the embarrassment you caused 'em in the first place.

He cleared his throat. Held out his hand. 'Reverend Jenkins. Richard. What I'm trying very, *very* badly to say is, the Church is holding a dance on Saturday night in a bid to attract some younger members to our congregation. I don't know if you've seen the posters—'

'Rock and roll.'

Couldn't miss 'em. Plastered over every wall and arch and bombed-out building, presumably because bill posters was only prosecuted if the perpetrator of this heinous crime was someone other than a man of the cloth.

'Good because the, um, the thing is, Miss Sneed, it seems you have quite a reputation when it comes to the jitterbug—'

And other things besides, I thought, but you know the Yanks, and what was said about them during the War. *Over sexed, overpaid, and over here.* Maybe they was, but Dolly Sneed always had a brand new pair of nylons, didn't she? Wore pretty shoes, the latest fashions, swung a handbag stuffed with Hershey bars, all at a time when everything from jam to milk to chocolate and tinned fruit was rationed, and the government only allowed you one measly egg a week. So up yours, all you snotty little cows who laughed at me in class, and wouldn't let me join your stupid little cliques. Not so stuck-up after that, were you? In your ugly, ration-book frocks and pencil lines down the back of your legs, to make it look like stockings. Who had the last laugh *then?*

'—so I was wondering if you, er, know anything about this new dance craze? Might teach me how to do it?'

And that's how it started, Richard and me. Us rocking and rolling in an empty hall to Elvis Presley's *It's All Right, Mama* (another bloomin' Yank!), perfecting our moves to Bill Hayley and Fats Domino, so he could show a bunch of teenagers that God was cool and church was fun. And I could show a bunch of frumps from school that I still had "it", and not just that.

That I had "it" in spades.

Unlike them, I'd kept me figure. The Americans, bless their generous hearts, were still flying their B-26s and B-29s out of Bovingdon back then, and though I never actually saw Clark Gable or Bob Hope wandering round Watford during the War, I caught a glimpse of James Stewart one time (least, I think it was him), and I'm pretty sure that bloke outside the dairy was William Holden. Spitting image from the back. That walk, you know...? The point being, you never knew who you might bump into. Maybe get a lucky break in Hollywood, or even British films.

Which is fine when you're eighteen. Not so fine when you're knocking thirty, not going steady or even courting, and are what the government deem a spinster and your old schoolfriends call an old maid.

Richard wasn't stupid. But at the same time, despite the War, or perhaps because of it, he wasn't very worldly, either. Pretty girl, witty, unconventional, independent, naturally men would be attracted to her like moths to a flame, but—

'What you have to understand, luv, is that these men were married, and married men get lonely.'

Wouldn't you, I added, giving him my well-rehearsed shudder at the horror of being stationed half a world from home, not knowing if you'd ever see your wife and kids again, or even live to see the sunset.

'That's all it ever was, though. Companionship. At a time when them boys needed it the most.'

At which point, his eyes welled up, he grasped both my hand. that was "the warmest, most wonderful, selfless act of charity he'd ever ... of", then dropped to his knees and promptly begged me to marry him.

I ask you. Who'd say no to that?

There were changes. Obviously. Stiletto heels were out. Not the right image, the bishop felt, which was a laugh, considering his penchant for patting little girls' bums. I scaled back on the port and brandies, learned to say "isn't" instead of "ain't", and how not to drop me "h's", but ooh, I didn't half miss sashaying around in them tight halternecks à la Sophia Loren! Tailored suits and button-to-the-collar blouses made me feel I was being strangled by a python, and between you and me, I'd have given anything to go striding down the High Street with Richard on me arm in a wife-beater t-shirt and denim jeans, like Marlon Brando in *A Streetcar Named Desire*. Not that Richard had the muscles. Or the pout. Or the passion, come to that. But a girl can dream, can't she? Besides. The War had been over ten long years, the bloom on my skin was slipping away, along with my options, and crikey. I'd put up with a bloody sight worse for a half-decent pair of nylons and a can of condensed milk.

What you need to remember, too, is that a vicar's wife carried a certain cachet in those days. Because now when I stepped out, it was Mrs. Jenkins this and Mrs. Jenkins that, and people made time for me, can you believe it? They'd actually stop me in the street to chat. Church stuff, as you'd expect. But still. They stopped. Showed respect for the first time I remember, and as though an invisible hand had flicked a switch, suddenly there was no more sniggering about my name, my nose, my whiny voice and lack of table manners. Dolly Sneed was Someone. Mrs. Someone, at that. So they could stick their ugly babies, bawling in their cheap perambulators, and their rented council houses, and their ugly husbands with work-rough hands and beery breath. Stick it where the postmen don't deliver letters.

No more being lied to. No more used, abused and treated with contempt by GI Joe. I mattered now. And guess what? I enjoyed it.

Thank you, thank you, Little Richard, and your beauti tutti fruitti.

· · · ·

WITH ME, OF COURSE, nothing good ever lasts for long. I should have known. That first winter, less than six months into our marriage, Richard (my Richard, not Little Richard!) went down with pneumonia. This wasn't new. He'd had it as a kid, three times as it happens. Left him with a weak chest, which is why he wasn't eligible to fight, and all credit to him, rocking round the clock to show the kids at the church dance that God was cool, even though it left him wheezing with a wracking cough for days. But if you think wearing prissy clothes and making polite conversation was not my forte, don't even think about my nursing skills. Patience, I'm sorry to say, was most definitely not one of my virtues in them days. Still isn't, come to that.

But.

For better or worse and all that—and let's face it. Marriage to the Rev. Someone was a million times better than being an old maid and working in the Co-op. So once again I astounded everybody in the parish (myself included) by making soup and filling hot water bottles, carefully mixing lemon with honey, washing him, helping him to the toilet, holding him while he hacked to bleeding point. At the time, I felt sure I deserved a medal. Or at the very least, a sainthood. "March 3rd, St. Dolly's Day". Nice ring to it, don't you think? Because despite the advances in penicillin, Richard took a week to ditch the fever, a month before the chest pain and the mucus had died down, and another couple of months before the fatigue cleared away and he was back to giving sermons and going on his rounds.

His flock, I have to say, were bleedin' marvellous. They brought round stews, cakes and home-baked bread, they pitched in with the gardening—weeds don't half sprout in springtime!—leaving presents on the hall table, and not just for the vicar. For the vicar's wife, can you imagine that! A bag of parma violets. Embroidered handkerchiefs. A pair of white lace gloves. In my entire life, no one had given me anything without a quid pro quo, and hand on heart, I was touched. Especially when the only way to catch my mum's attention was to steal money from her purse, kick the paint off the front door, or beat up my tittle-tattle of a sister, because even a clout round the ear and a night in the coal cellar without supper meant she was making time for me.

'Do you have any idea of how hard it is, being a widow and raising two kids on yer own?' she'd yell.

'Not so 'ard, you can't keep a bottle of gin glued to yer lips,' I'd yell back.

That constituted conversation as far as my mother and me was concerned. I don't recall her ever hugging me, even when I had me tonsils out. No, the best I had to look forward to was Christmas, with an orange, a few walnuts, and a bar of soap that was not carbolic. While birthdays meant a new liberty bodice and a bag of toffees, which I was meant to share. Dream on.

Of course, they're both gone now, my mother and my sister. Bombed out in 1940, the week I ran away from home.

Who knows? Perhaps there is a God?

• • • •

'YOU SHOULD HAVE BEEN a cat, you know that, don't you?'

Richard was just back from his weekly tour of the sick, the poor, the dying, the bereaved. I was at the dining room table, head down over me new Singer sewing machine, because that's another skill I didn't know I had. The ability to make me own clothes. And I was good at pinning on the paper patterns, cutting out the fabric, tacking, hemming, pinking, sewing seams. I was. A skill, admittedly, which sprung from my desire (some might say obsession) with trawling through them great, big pattern books in the department stores. *Vogue* being my favourite, but give me a *Butterick* or a *McCalls* and I'd be lost for days. Drooling over film star evening gowns with fish-tail hems and off-the-shoulder necklines, or big, wide skirts, be-bop-a-lula, and skin-tight pants like Audrey Hepburn wore in *Funny Face*.

'Own up, Richard Jenkins. Who was it snitched about how I spend my time curled up at the foot of the bed when you're out?'

He laughed. Kissed me on the ear, having missed my mouth because I needed to fix a seam that needed unexpectedy re-pinning. 'Secrets of the confessional, I'm afraid.' He slumped down in the armchair. 'But the thing about you, Dolly, and the reason I say that, is that no matter how hard you try, you'll never be totally domesticated.'

'You called in on that Miss Cox again, didn't yer?' For all I'd turned my lips away, I was smiling. 'How many of the furry monsters does she have now? Four?'

'Six, but she's eighty-two and lonely,' he said, picking a scrap of ginger fur off his trouser leg. 'She deserves all the love she can get at her age.'

'And you deserve a cup of tea at yours, luv.'

'I'll give you a hand.'

'You'll sit in that armchair and read the paper, Richard Jenkins.' Back end of May, and the colour was only just coming back in his cheeks. 'I am the cat that walks by itself and all places are alike to me, remember?'

'Even the kitchen?'

'Especially the kitchen.'

By the time I'd made the tea, he was fast asleep.

• • • •

AFTER THE PNEUMONIA, there was no more *awap-bop-a-lu-bop awap-bam-bam* in the church hall for us. No shake, rattle and rolling. No stepping on anyone's blue suede shoes. Of course we still tuned our wireless to Radio Luxembourg of an evening. At least those evenings when Richard wasn't at church meetings, taking choir practice or running Beetle drives. Which, I might add, I avoided like the plague.

'You ought to come,' he'd say. 'They're fun.'

Fun? Rolling dice to pin different body parts to insects?

'Next time,' I'd say, with a twinkle in my eye. He knew I was happier alone with the record player, bopping round the living room while the jailhouse rocked and Guy Mitchell never felt more like singing the blues. I think, deep down inside, he also sensed that his parishioners were happier, too. That without me there, a non-believer in believer's clothing, they breathed more easily. Hypocrisy always finds its level.

But life after illness finds its level, too, and me, I found another skill. Organising things, jumble sales in particular. Again, not my first choice, but when Mrs. Meredith had a stroke, someone needed to step in, and I don't care who called me bossy, rigid, rhymes-with-witch, I got the job done, didn't I? That year, the Church banked a third more in takings, which was a terrific boost for Richard's new soup kitchen project, so you can shut your ugly faces, all you back-biters from school, and remember who it was that raised more food in that year's Harvest Festival than any that had gone before it.

And so what, a bit of swearing slipped out there?

No one's bleedin' perfect.

As for Richard, well...slower songs meant slower dances, and what's wrong with clicking your fingers to Blueberry Hill or tapping your toes from the sofa while someone went sneakin' round the corner, could that someone be Mack the Knife? The Clean Air Act meant a new gas fire downstairs, a two-bar electric in the bedroom, and that autumn we was as warm as toast, drinking the cheap sherry the bishop and his boring wife brought round, watching the brand new ITV channel, playing Monopoly, and going to the pictures.

But like I said, when it comes to Dolly Sneed, nothing good lasts long.

Richard, poor bugger, caught the flu.

• • • •

EXCUSE MY SWEARING, but holy bleedin' *!?~*!!*, 'cause if you think pneumonia's bad, this was ten times worse. First off, his temperature shot through the roof. Scary enough, but add on chills, joint pain, diarrhoea (that was just the tip of the iceberg), and I'd never known so many heart-stopping moments in me life. Considering the epidemic started the year before, I suppose he was lucky not to have caught it then. "Asian flu" they called it. Something to do with ducks, don't know what exactly, but I do know three and a half thousand people in Britain died from it—and when you're prone to bronchial pneumonia, I swear the Pearly Gates creaked open half a dozen times.

• • • •

ONCE AGAIN, THOUGH, his parish proved terrific. Even though he was laid up in hospital, they brought round pies and soups and stews and pasties for me, baked flapjacks, swiss rolls and macaroons, and swamped the entire house with flowers. This was wintertime, remember, and the sacrifices them poor people made to buy me roses, violets, lilies, freesias, brought a lump to my throat. Their scent lingered right the way to June.

The women, bless 'em, knitted shawls for the vicar's wife, an Aran cardi for the reverend. Their husbands mowed the lawn, checked out the electrics and the plumbing, replaced two washers on the taps, and re-painted the kitchen and the lounge. As for the books they donated, dear me, I'm sure we ended up with more than the local public library, but you won't hear Dolly Sneed complain. Believe me, when you're nursing an invalid back to health, time passes slower than a snail without its shell.

Leastways, for active girls like me.

I drank too much, I must admit, and sod the port, just gimme the bloody brandy. But the bottle and the books between 'em saved my sanity, because what's that saying? *Them what never reads live only one life. Them what do live a thousand.* Glutton that I was, I guzzled everything from pulp fiction to biographies, via serious literature and lurid magazines. National Geographic was my lifeline. Without 'em, see, it was just me and the Courvoisier, taking me back to days when strong arms pulled me, laughing, on to the dance floor, and I'd jive and jitterbug until the music stopped, Glenn Miller still ringing in me ears as the same strong arms pulled me down. That's when I'd close the living room door, so Richard upstairs in bed wouldn't hear, and blast out things like *Boogie Woogie Bugle Boy* and *In the Mood,* where Courvoisier and I could pretend I was wearing strappy shoes with a little bow on top, and that frilly skirt that showed my petticoats and sometimes more, while men whistled, clapped and cheered.

· · · ·

'AND HE BEGAN REASONING to himself, saying, "What shall I do, since I have no place to store my crops?"'

'Funny, I thought the delirium had passed a month ago.'

'Next Sunday's sermon,' Richard said, smiling. 'Luke 12, 16-21, the parable of the rich man, whose land was proving remarkably productive. *Then he said, "This is what I will do. I will tear down my barns and build larger ones, and there I will store all my grain and my goods. And I will say to my soul, Soul, you have many goods laid up for many years to come; take your ease, eat, drink and be merry. But God said to the rich man, "You fool! This very night your soul is required of you, and now who will own what you have prepared?" So is the man who stores up treasure for himself, and is not rich toward God."*'

'God said that?'

'His exact words.'

My turn to laugh. 'Why are you telling me this?' I shot a comical glance over my shoulder. 'Did God tell you, in his exact words, that the Grim Reaper's creeping up, about to swing his sickle any second?'

He smiled, but this time it didn't reach his eyes. 'I'm worried, Dolly. In less than a dozen years, people seem to have forgotten the horrors and the deprivations of war and—'

'You worry too much, Richard Jenkins. That's what you do. You spend too much time out there in the parish—'

'I'm their minister. They need me.'

'I need you, too, luv. You're hardly ever home.'

And when he was, it was only because he'd picked up a tummy bug from Sunday school, or shingles from a kid with chicken pox. Trust me, if it was going round, he'd catch it. In fact, his resistance was so bleedin' low, a common cold would lay him low for weeks, but God bless 'em, his flock never let up. Loved him like a son, they did, so even when one illness rolled into another and he was bedridden half the time, they'd bake round the clock, knit, sew, make the prettiest lace outside Flanders, and you know the funny thing? They didn't do it out of duty, boredom or any of the reasons I'd have done it for. They did it 'cause they liked me. Imagine that! Dolly Sneed, Mrs. Popular. Who'd have thought it, eh?

That's when I started pressing some of the flowers. Not the likes of Joe Mackenzie's roses or Miss Hemmings' potted cyclamen. I didn't need no physical reminders of *their* generosity and help. I'm talking about the pansies, violets, even that sprig of mimosa sent round by the girls I went to school with. And when they'd dried properly, squashed between the mammoths and the manatees in the *Encyclopedia of Mammals,* I propped them upright on my writing bureau, like pupils in class, so I could look at 'em, standing in a line, and say, *well, girls. Never thought you'd be bringing me flowers, did yer? Not when you was teasing me about not knowing how to calculate, or when I got my Keats all wrong and called it "myths and mellow fruitfulness", or 'cause I couldn't tell my acids from my alkali. Who's top of the class now, eh? You answer that.*

• • • •

I CAN'T BEGIN TO DESCRIBE what it was like when Richard died, and so I won't.

'It probably started with him straining his back loading sacks for famine relief in Ethiopia', the doctor said, adding, under his breath and off the record, that the tramps who called at the soup kitchen carried all manner of infectious diseases. With his immunity at rock bottom, the poor bugger stood no chance (my words there, not his), and him at only forty-two years old.

Oh, it was a lovely funeral, though. Folk turned out from miles around, not a dry eye to be seen, and I got so much sympathy from everyone—so brave, they said, leading that horse-drawn procession with dignity and pride—I thought I'd die myself from all that hugging. For two weeks, I was inundated with the same thoughtful gifts and food baskets...then the new vicar arrived. Equally young, equally enthusiastic, but this one came with a wife of his own. A snotty little cow, who looked down her ugly, pointy nose at girls what dropped their "h's". Even though she tried hard not to show it, I could sense it. Saw it in her smile, the condescending rhymes-with-witch.

I knew that after Richard died, I wouldn't be allowed to live in the rectory. But in my mind, I was convinced they—the church in general, the bishop in particular—would find a house for me. God knows, they owned enough property in the area, but no. Turfed out on my ear I was, and not a single petition from the people of the parish.

Not one.

Hurt? To the bleedin' bone I was. Angrier than a hornets nest on fire, but what could I do? Women had no rights back then. A vicar's stipend paid sod-all, and while Richard left me everything he owned, his worldly goods, when cashed in at the pawn shop, came to less than fifty quid. Luckily, I'd stashed a bit aside. Surprising amount of good stuff hidden in amongst that jumble, and the money I'd saved on the housekeeping with all those pies and pastries, well I gave half to Richard, 'cause he knew we was in credit, but half I put away for a rainy day.

Now look. Bloody pissing down.

Excuse my French.

I went to London. Obviously. The lure of the bright lights and all that, and for the same reason I chose a town near the American airforce base during the War, I headed straight to Hammersmith for its famous Palais. And why not?

The strain of dosing Richard round the clock, keeping a close eye on him as he faded day by day, had took its toll, and hells bells, I was only thirty-bleedin'-six. So then, all you gone-to-seed fat lumps from school, know this. Dolly Sneed was still a looker, because crikey, you should have seen them heads turn when I walked in the bar. Elvis might have been lonesome tonight, I wasn't. More Helen Shapiro, me. Walking back to happiness, *woopah oh yeah yeah*.

• • • •

BUT—AND STOP ME IF you've heard this one before—nothing good EVER lasts for long where I'm concerned. Four months after Richard died, I'd gorged myself knock-kneed on fashion, wore my hair longer and in flick-ups, and was twisting the night away like you wouldn't believe on the bounciest dance floor in England. But a girl's gotta live, ai—*hasn't* she? Being a vicar's wife (make that widow) counted for nothing. All I could find was shop work, and the pay from that don't go far. Not at the centre of the universe, anyway. No, what I needed was a man. Someone to look after me, and although time was knocking on, it wasn't too late for me to have kids, make some bloke a proud and happy dad.

His name was Johnny, and he was everything the Reverend Richard Jenkins wasn't. Tall, muscular, dark and broody, he was seven years younger than me, rode a motorbike, and boy, did Johnny's blood run red. Wild times, baby. Wild, wild times. We drank too much, popped little pills, rode full throttle on the open road, not caring if we lived or died, yeeha. Oh, could that man dance! I've never known anyone with so much stamina, both in and out of bed. Makes me shiver thinking about it, even now. He was a bricklayer, and bricklayers earned good money in the late '50s/early '60s. Dolly Sneed was jiving down Easy Street now and she was happy. At least—

'What the—'

'*Shit.*'

'You said you was working overtime, you lying cheating bastard!'

I was yelling at Johnny, but at the same time dragging that bitch out of my bed by her long, blonde, back-combed hair, and you know the best thing about middle-class teenage girls? No idea how to fight.

'Babe. I'm sorry. I thought you were going to the Palais tonight.'

'I had a headache—' kick, slap, punch '—left early—' throw intruder naked out the door '—came home in time to catch my man with some ugly, two-bit hooker.' Toss clothes out front window, into the street.

Johnny promised, on his mother's grave, he wouldn't stray again. Blamed her, the booze, the purple hearts, but swore, on bended knee, it was the worst mistake he'd ever made.

The worst mistake *I* ever made was believing him.

Blondie wasn't the first, but what hurt—what really cut me to the marrow—was that wasn't the first time for them. They'd been at it for over a month, creeping behind my back, shagging in my bed, and how did I find out? Johnny Subtle packed my bags and piled them in the lounge.

'I'm sorry, Babe, it's just not working out for us.'

'That's all you have to say?'

'It was good while it lasted, but I've found someone else. Just give me the key, Babe. Don't make a scene.'

At that point, I knew why he called me Babe. He called all his women Babe, that way he never got their names mixed up. Didn't even need to remember 'em, the bastard.

That was also the point where, in pulp fiction, they say the red mist descends. Red be buggered. This was white hot anger. In the space of thirty seconds, I let rip with every ounce of ammunition in the store. I called him names, I smashed his plates, I told him what I thought of his leaving dirty socks littered round the floor and his rotten taste in shoes. I screamed because he lied, I screamed because he cheated, I screamed because she was young enough to be my bloody daughter, and had perfect little tits. And when he grabbed me by the wrists and said, 'Calm down, or else I'll call the police,' I spat at him and hissed, 'Just try, just you bloody try, because if I killed one man, don't think I won't kill you, either, Johnny Kelly.'

• • • •

EXACTLY.

Me and my big mouth.

Of course, I tried to laugh it off. Blamed him, the booze, the purple hearts. Swore on my mother's grave it was a joke. A bad joke, sure, but one made in the heat of the moment. Broken heart and all that, Sergeant.

The police didn't *not* believe me.

But they needed to be sure.

Three days later, an exhumation order saw the Rev. Jenkins rising from his grave way ahead of Judgment Day. A post-mortem examination revealed large amounts of arsenic in the body.

· · · ·

'COULD BE ANYONE,' I wailed. 'All them cakes and pies and pastries.'

'But you weren't ill from eating them, were you? There's no trace of arsenic in your system, either.'

Something to do with hair, apparently. You can test for it in hair, and mine was clear.

'We also found this article, Mrs. Jenkins. Marked up, and hidden deep in your belongings.'

Bloody stupid of me, that, and you know the silly thing? The only reason I hung on to that bleedin' paper—the one featuring the Angel Makers of Nagyrév—was 'cause I was worried about leaving it in the rectory/in the jumble/even in the dustbin, in case someone—the new vicar's wife/Mrs. Meredith (on her feet after the stroke)/one of Richard's tramps rummaging through the rubbish—might put two and two together.

God knows, I didn't take much with me. None of those frumpy python-squeezers, that's for sure. But I couldn't risk leaving any evidence behind, so I slipped it in among me records, intending to throw it away in Hammersmith, but because dance moved on from rock and roll to twist and I was no longer living in the past, I forgot about it. I ask you. How daft's that?

You probably don't know about the Angel Makers. I didn't neither, till I read it in the papers, but it was around the turn of the century it started. In Hungary, in case I hadn't said, when a midwife turned up in some remote farming village, a widow, though no one there had ever met or knew the husband. Gawd knows how he died. Anyway, as well as delivering babies and generally healing people (there being no resident doctors in remote farming villages), this woman performed abortions. Which, of course, was as illegal then as they are now, and though she was arrested a dozen times or more, no judge felt inclined to imprison her for what they themselves supported.

So far, so good, but then the Great War kicked off, didn't it? The men went off to fight (not sure which side), while prisoners-of-war were held in nearby camps and tasked with working the land in the farmers' absence. Well, you don't need to be a genius to guess what happened next. Women, married off as teenage brides to husbands chosen for them, quickly found a strong-backed outlet for their repression. And when the war was over, they reasoned there had to be an alternative to the old days of subjugation. Especially when a number of their husbands were abusive alcoholics, and divorce was not an option.

This is where the midwife came into her own. She boiled the arsenic off strips of fly-paper and sold it (120 *penges* down, 120 more after the funeral, another 120 when the estate was settled) to whoever needed it. Which, it seemed, was pretty much everyone! It was said three hundred people were poisoned by the ladies of Nagyrév, but that sounds an awful lot for one remote farming village. One thing's for sure, though. Of the fifty bodies that was dug up, forty-six contained arsenic. Hence the name, the Angel Makers.

'I never bought a gramme of arsenic in my life,' I protested at the trial. 'You ask any of the chemists. Not one bleedin' grain.'

'You did buy fly papers, though, did you not?' Oh he was smarmy, that QC. Thought he had me there.

'We was plagued with flies, ask anyone. What with the orchard at the back.' Take that!

'And so you used, what? Ten fly papers a day, every day? One an hour?'

I can hear the laughter from the gallery, even now. Same horsey snorts I remembered oh-so-well from school, when I fumbled with my protractor and compasses, couldn't draw for toffees, and was hauled up before Headmaster for telling tales on Phyllis Hall and Joycie White. Yeah, well, laugh away, 'cause how many of *them* could have done their husbands in and not been caught?

Like I said. Me and my big mouth.

• • • •

YOU THINK I DID IT because of the excitement, don't you? That I was sick of cutting paper patterns, rifling through fusty attic throwaways, wearing collars that made you feel like you had a noose around your neck. Wrong. Boring, all that small talk, I'll agree. But that was the life I'd chosen, I was happy with my lot. Me and Richard, shake, rattling and rolling until his chest became too weak, and he threw his reduced energies into building up parish activities with things like beetle drives and relief funds. All good works I grant you, and people loved him for it—and that's the point. They loved me too. Not in the same way. Obviously. But once one illness rolled into another then another, that weren't no life for him, poor sod. He was better off out of it, he really was. And I swear to God, on my dear mother's grave, Richard didn't suffer. Leastways, no worse than all the things he'd gone through a dozen times before, so he was used to it when you look at it like that—and come on. With all them pies and tarts and soups and stews, there were so many opportunities to slip the arsenic in, and the doctor, bless his cotton socks, did not suspect a thing. (Strained back indeed!)

I honestly believed that, when Richard was gone and there was no more holding sick bowls under him or helping him on and off the toilet, his parishioners would look out for the Widow Jenkins. That they'd find a little house for me, bring me gifts and food, and I'd return the favour by pitching in with beetle drives and stuff. I would. Give back some of the kindness they'd given me, because when it boils down to it, we all want to be loved, don't we?

Instead, I'm lying in the dark with nothing for company except the cold, my memories of Richard, and that long slow dance through the passage of time.

An owl hoots from the ancient, spreading oak. Voles rustle through the fallen leaves along the hedgerow. The bell of St. Giles tolls four.

I'd known my grave would be this lonely, I'd have asked to be cremated.

C athy never really wanted much out of life. Good health. Good legs. A good man to love, and who would love her in return. OK, maybe a few other things, too, like good wine, good skin, good weather, and of course, a good book to curl up with on the sofa would round it off nicely. As would the time to sit down and write novels. Thrillers. All right, maybe not thrillers, but suspense, though. Something with a bit of a—you know. Bite.

She most certainly didn't hanker after Versace, Louis Vuitton or Jimmy Choo, any more than she needed yachts or mansions or first class Virgin flights to the Caribbean to make her happy, although she wouldn't have turned her nose up at any of those. No way, José. Uh-uh. But comfort, oh yes, comfort would be nice, ditto a career that didn't involve any of the suffocating restrictions imposed on Civil Servants.

'Interfacing with the public's great,' she'd tell her friends. 'The job's secure, the hours are fine, and I can't complain about the salary.'

'But...?'

'But nothing,' she would lie. 'It's brilliant.'

Brilliant, providing you like having your initiative stifled twenty times an hour. Even better, if you enjoy working in the kind of silence that makes libraries rowdy in comparison. And absolutely dazzling, if you're the sort who enjoys repetition, because there's nothing like working in the Country Records Office when it comes to repetition. Birth, deaths and marriages. Not a lot of room for manoeuvre there, where even the ink to sign the certificates is a special non-fade blend.

'What you need, Cath, is excitement.'

'Adventure.'

'A hot, passionate romance.'

Prosecco is famous for giving wise counsel.

'And where exactly will I find excitement, adventure and a hot, passionate lover?' she laughed. 'Not with a father registering his daughter's birth, thank you very much! Or some old man, his shaking hand clutching the form from the hospital where his wife passed away. Or would you girls have me snogging the groom at the back of the Register Office?'

'Try internet dating.'

'Cruise the supermarket aisles on a Friday after work.'

'If the old man was rolling in it, I'd say give it a go.'

The second bottle of Prosecco tends to lack the same wisdom, the third even more so, but we shall skip over that. The point is that, as spring turned into summer then faded to autumn, Cathriona's wish list grew fatter, rather than longer.

Good health still topped the list, but for the first time, she'd begun to notice that when work colleagues fell ill, the delay in treatment became crucial in fighting disease, and that kind of response only came through private health cover. Good wine had become subtly defined by vintages that were always £10 a bottle ahead of her budget, no matter how much she paid. While good legs, even at the ripe old age of thirty-six, needed cash thrown at them, either from bronzing or waxing or sessions at the gym, and the same applied to maintaining a healthy complexion. Bottom line: the money just didn't go as far as it used to.

And while she had ample time (way too much time, actually) to curl up on the sofa with the latest bestseller, any attempts at novel writing fell flat. The plots were limp, the characters lifeless. What was needed was in-depth research of her exotic settings to make the damn things jump off the page. To travel business—no, first class!—the way her protagonists did. What a pity luxury wasn't compatible with a Civil Service pay grade.

'You need a sugar daddy, Cath.'

'Or a hot date.'

'Or a cat to wrap round your neck, purr on your pillow, and weave in and out of your ankles.'

'Two's better, then they'll have some kitty companionship.'

'Make that three.'

'OK, but four at the most.'

See what I mean about that last bottle of Prosecco? In fact, Cathriona was still smiling the following morning, when Kevin came to register his addict brother's death, and boy, was he easy to talk to. As an only child, she knew what it was like to be an orphan, completely alone in the world. He was glad someone else understood. Working in contract law for a company that built food processing plants, he knew all about rules and regulations, stifled initative, the straightjacket constraints of a job in which no i's were more dotted, no t's ever more crossed. One date rolled into many.

Even so, it was a while before she told her friends about Kevin.

'Is he hot?'

'Is he witty?'

'Is he rich?'

Hot wasn't the word that instantly sprang to mind. Average height, average build, hair neither light nor dark, neither curly nor straight, clothes neither trendy or stuffy.

'He has this cute little dimple in his chin,' Cathriona told them. 'And you know that song by the Pointer Sisters? *I want a man with a slow hand...?*'

Cue a predictable chorus of oohs and aahs, and you lucky cow, followed, of course, by another bottle of fizz.

'What about the witty bit?'

'He's caring,' Cathy said. 'Compassionate. Thoughtful.'

One of the first things he said to her was *tell me the things you hate about yourself, so I can start loving them.*

'Never mind all that stuff, is he RICH?'

'Most definitely not,' she said firmly.

But he could be. Oh, yes, how he could be...

And from that moment on, Cathriona made sure her friends knew exactly how devoted she was, how deeply in love. Every time they met up, she gushed about the bird house he built for her, the meals he cooked, the way he always opened the car door for her. His eyes were the greenest, his laughter infectious, and—

'—you should hear his Clint Eastwood *go ahead, make my day* impression!'

It was important, correction, it was critical, that they knew she was ape-shit crazy for him. Couldn't imagine life without this man in it.

So it was a little surprising, given all the gushing, that it wasn't until her wedding day (after the Dirty Harry *go ahead, make my day* impression) that her friends learned of Kevin's penchant for extreme sports.

'Why didn't you tell us?' they cried.

'Laugh and the world laughs with you,' she said. 'Worry, and you bring everyone down.'

Bungee jumping, paragliding, free-diving and motocross were oxygen to her husband. Ice climbing, for those times when rock climbing wasn't enough of a rush. Show him a kayak and a stretch of boiling rapids, and he was orgasmic.

'But these are dangerous sports,' her friends cried out in horror.

Tell her something she didn't already know.

• • • •

'WE SHOULD TAKE OUT life insurance,' Cathriona announced, during their honeymoon.

Two warm, sunny weeks in north-central Florida, which he spent cave-diving, and she spent next to a sparkling blue pool, writing about a filthy rich socialite being terrorized by her neighbour, in a bid to drive her insane so she could claim the husband for herself.

(Good weather, remember, was also on Cathriona's Want List).

'Life insurance? What on earth for?' Kevin laughed off the notion. 'Don't you think I can still cut it at thirty-six?'

At which point he pounded his rock solid abs, yodelled like Tarzan, and promptly carried her off to the bedroom.

A month after coming home, though, having been bombarded with statistics ('every year, darling, in every *one* of these sports, there are over a hundred fatalities'), he finally agreed it made sense. Even so—

'How much?' Green eyes stood out on stalks, when she showed him the contracts. 'Jeez, Cath, if anything happens, you'll be the richest widow in history!'

'Or you'll be the richest widower.'

An unlikely scenario.

Extreme spell-checking still hadn't caught on.

• • • •

STILL. LOVE, AS THEY keep telling us, is a many-splendoured thing, so it was no great surprise that Cathriona should want to bone up on her husband's energetic pursuits. All right, *Paragliding Weekly* was strictly for nerds, but *The Only Way is Ice* wasn't too stodgy, and *Rock On!* a lot better than its covers suggested. But it was *Down & Dirty,* a twice-monthly cave-diving magazine, that really caught her attention.

Three times she read the article all the way through. Pored over the photos of Gabriel Field, a tall, bronzed man in his forties, geography teacher by profession, marathon runner for charity, with several hundred dives under his belt. Gabriel Field had a wife and three children, and the images of their empty faces at his memorial service would haunt Cathriona for months.

Memorial service, for the simple reason they never recovered his body.

According to *Down & Dirty*, there's no place on the planet with as many underwater caves as the Yucatan Peninsula. Over a hundred different cave entrances, leading to mile upon mile of tunnels, each adorned with spectacular stalactites, stalagmites and columns. To a geography teacher, this would have been catnip.

Gabriel's dive buddy, his face wracked with pain, explained how they'd been laying a line to guide themselves out, when the reel jammed. As always in situations like this, you turn back straight away, and Gabriel indicated that he was behind him. The trouble was, the caves of the Yucatan are shallow in comparison, and although the dive buddy was equally experienced, his knowledge of caverns was thin. To make matters worse, his primary light failed.

'I did the one thing a diver must never do,' he told the magazine. 'I panicked.'

He didn't stop to consider that, if his back up-light failed this deep into the underground system, Gabriel had both primary and back-up lights, and they would be safe. Panic invariably overrides logic, and consequently, instead of using finning techniques that would prevent the fine silt on the floor from swirling up, he swam as fast as he could to safety. It was only when he reached the cave mouth that he realized the reason he couldn't see Gabriel behind him had nothing to do with the haziness of the water, and after a few minutes, he began to get worried.

'I mean, really worried, man.'

He checked his air supply and noticed it was getting low. Which meant Gabriel's would have been, too.

Having screwed up once, he was determined not to panic a second time. Fully equipped, and with a spare tank for Gabriel, the dive buddy followed the line back into the caves. Swirling sediment or not, Gabriel was experienced enough to be able to track the line home. What went wrong?

The general consensus was catnip. That, as a geography teacher, he had been so taken by the beauty of these watery tunnels, that he had fallen victim to the same compulsion that drives most of us. The desire to see what's round the next corner. Just the next one, the next one, just one more then—

There's a saying, the magazine article said, *that watching your air pressure drop to zero is no way to spend the rest of your life.*

Yet it would appear that was exactly what happened to Gabriel Field. He became lost in the labyrinth, and his air ran out long before he found the line laid by their reel. His body was never found.

Cave diving in Mexico is not like cave diving in Florida, the magazine said. *For one thing, forget four-wheel drives, you need burros. You're tracking a long way through jungle, and even with maps, it's hard to know how far to go or where to turn, many sites are difficult to find, few of the cave entrances have signs, and those that do are often misleading. Unless you speak fluent Spanish, you won't just be in for a rude awakening. You're risking your life, and those of others.*

Cathriona looked over to where her husband was watching the rugby, England v. Wales in the finals.

'How do you fancy a trip to the Yucatan Peninsular, Kevin?'

• • • •

CATHY'S FRIENDS WERE not remotely surprised when she quit her job after her husband's death, upped sticks, and moved to Australia. Sydney was as far removed from her old life as it was possible to get, both geographically and in the way of life there. They wished her nothing but luck.

All she'd ever wanted, they said, was a good man to love, and to be loved in return.

• • • •

NOT ENTIRELY.

She'd wanted good health. Check. Good legs. Check. Good weather, check, check check, and dear god, wines don't come much better than Barossa Valley, especially the '99, '98 and '96 vintage.

Sitting by the pool—her own pool—overlooking Sanctuary Island in the Narabeen Lakes, and just metres away from the ocean, Cathriona leaned back in her chair and stretched.

'Novel going well, love?'

'Zipping along,' she said, which it was. Sod those ridiculous socialites being slowly driven insane. She always said she'd wanted to write something with a bit of bite, and nothing bit quite like rampant werewolves and naked vampires. Publishers couldn't get enough of her erotic romances, this was already her fifth bestseller, and climbing.

She couldn't have done any of this, if she hadn't killed Kevin.

If *they* hadn't killed Kevin.

Her eyes ran over his rippling muscles as he towelled himself dry. 'You want me to read you this latest chapter?'

Green eyes danced. 'Go ahead, make my day.'

Yes, she'd wanted all those other things, but at the top of her list was a good man to love, and to be loved in return. From the moment they met, Kevin was that man, and together, they hatched a plan.

Theoretically, "Kevin" was dead. Lost in a watery labyrinth below the Yucatan jungle, a tragedy of unimaginable proportions for the wife who loved him with all her heart. But though they both now called him Adam, that dimple in his chin remained unbearably sexy, those green eyes still sparkled with mischief, and Sydney offered all the surfing a man could ever need.

In the background the Pointer Sisters played out.

'I want a man with a slow hand...'

On her lap, a cat purred contentedly, while another wove in and out of her ankles.

SAW POINT

Inspector! Goodness gracious, what a wonderful surprise. Your lovely wife is well, I trust? And the boys? My, my, a girl as well now? Heartfelt felicitations to you sir, it just shows how time flies, does it not? Alas, it has been many months since The Great Rivorsky last performed here, in London. During that time our illustrious company has toured Paris, Athens, Berlin, Budapest, we were in Vienna when the poor Titanic went down last year...but heavens, where are my manners? Come in, come in. No, no, you are not at all disturbing me. Please. Take this chair beside the stove.

I confess, I had not expected to light a fire so early in the season, but then again, I had quite forgotten how foul your wretched fog can be at times. Swirls right into the bones. Even the best illusionist cannot make October turn into April with a swish of his wand, though, and in order to make elephants disappear and be able to shoot bullets for Pepé to catch in his teeth, his hands must remain flexible. Of course, this fine single malt whisky also goes some way towards achieving that objective, though I fear you are under a misapprehension regarding the warmth this lovely young lady was providing.

Being ten—very well, twenty years younger than I, Greta does not feel the same cold in her marrow and felt, therefore, compelled to remove certain garments to cool down, did you not, Greta, dear? As you are finding out for yourself, Inspector, for a pot-bellied stove, it emits a great deal of heat. Feel free to mop your brow with my handkerchief. I have them especially monogrammed at Harrods—ah. My apologies. That appears to be the young lady's stocking, though how it came to be in my waistcoat pocket is a mystery.

Now, Greta, I suggest you gather up your little frilly bits and run along. We will continue the interview for the post of levitation fairy tomorrow, which is the only reason, Inspector, the *only* reason I had my hands round her waist when you knocked. One needs to ascertain the circumference with a certain degree of precision. Passing the hoops round the levitated body to prove there are no wires and all that, because never let it be said the Great Rivorsky is less than professional.

Inventive, too, you say? Ha, ha, you have not forgotten the incident with the squirrel, then?

155

'You have so many doves, ducks and rabbits hidden in your greatcoat,' you told me at the time, 'it's a wonder you don't open a petting zoo between shows.'

Another whisky, Inspector? I think you will need the added refreshment when I relate the sad tale of the Siamese twins while I worked the Riviera this year. Sad, because there were none available for hire, but a true showman thinks on his feet, and for the first three performances we had no problems tying Mimi and Helga together inside a very large frock. My word, watching those girls, I was half convinced myself that they were conjoined.

Pure bad luck that the wind kicked up without warning, but you know *Le Mistral.* Comes in when it pleases, stays up to a week. Caught the hem of their skirt, whisked it right up, and there. Large as life and twice as shapely, two pairs of finely turned ankles. Did I say skirt? More like a mainsail. Our Helga lacks total control when faced with madeira cake. Indeed, any kind of cake, now I come to think of it, which is not always a disadvantage. True, she nearly crushed her third husband, poor fellow, but on more than one occasion I have had her stand in for the strong-man when he passed out from the drink, and quite honestly, Inspector, not a soul has noticed the difference.

But then, I run an illusion act, not a freak show—well, yes, you're quite right. I do currently employ a hermaphrodite and a man monkey, and exhibit a mummy, a lunatic and a two-headed calf, but only because the British public do so love their sideshows. And on a practical level, one needs some method of funding the transportation of caravans, personnel, backdrops and stage props, not forgetting, of course, the aforementioned elephant. Making a creature that size disappear is quite tricky. But not half as tricky as making the wretched thing cross the English Channel in winter.

Now, sir. Before there is no more fine malt left in this bottle, perhaps you would care to divulge the reason for your visit?

If it's last night's performance, I am more than willing to reimburse anyone affronted by that unfortunate incident. Alas, we encountered a problem with the second contortionist, and at this point I should draw your attention to our earlier conversation, in my capacity of not so much impressario as *improvisio.*

I assume you know how sawing the lady in half works? One contortionist climbs into the coffin, in which a second is already hidden. The toes that wriggle are of course the second lady, while Number One waves and smiles, occasionally grimacing for effect, while I saw the coffin in two.

What happened last night was that my toe-wriggler became extremely unwell immediately prior to the performance. Poor girl contracted a nasty case of pilfering, and I'm afraid she needed to be quarantined until she revealed the name of the pawnbroker to whom she sold Marguerite's locket, my mind reader's necklace and the elephant man's pocket watch. By which I mean the man who tends to the elephant, not Joseph Merrick, who died some twenty-odd years ago. The point, Inspector, is that as a result of her quarantine, there required some dedicated inventiveness on my part for the show to go on, which is why I substituted Pepé to hide in the coffin and wriggle his toes.

Pepé, you may recall, is a dwarf. Charming fellow, highly amusing, genial to a fault, and quite multi-talented, and I don't mind admitting that the Great Rivorsky would only be the Magnificent Rivorsky without him. What I failed to take into account were Pepé's ankles. They are far fatter than my contortionist's, who has the girth of a willow twig, and when his ankles became wedged...well, you see the problem, Inspector.

I am merrily playing the showman. With a swish of a cape here and a wave of a wand there, I return the two halves of the coffin to their joined position, my contortionist climbs out, even though her feet are still kicking like a bucking bronco from the far end of the box. Utter disaster. So if the local constabulary feel I have been defrauding the public by retaining their money, I assure you this is purely a short term, nay temporary, nay *provisional* situation until the coffers are flush again.

No, sir, not flush like these cards. Mere slip of the hand, that. Being a magician, I can't help it. One's hands move when one is nervous, and see? The Queen of Diamonds yet again. And in your top pocket this time.

Ah. Your visit is not connected to that unfortunate incident.

Murder, you say?

In which the Great Rivorsky can help the police with their enquiries?

• • • •

MILL HILL IS A DELIGHTFUL little village served by the Edgware, Highgate & London Railway, with a church built by William Wilberforce in between bouts of abolishing slavery. It also boasts a pond and a small green, around which cluster many quaint weatherboard cottages and more than one ale house. One of many settlements that sprang up along an ancient, if not prehistoric, thoroughfare, its open space, fresh air and quacking ducks must make for a most agreeable existence.

It is not, however, conducive to theatrical performances of a lively and, dare I say it, titillating nature.

Tea, Inspector? Although I must say you had me going there, you and your little joke. Helping the police with their enquiries, indeed! Of course you are right. Who else but another illusionist would be able to dissemble the trick you describe, and thus determine whether the deceased met her end as a result of an unfortunate accident. Or something colder and far, far more sinister.

There you go. A nice strong cup of English tea. Just the thing for this vile fog, especially since the last of the whisky slipped through my hands with the shock. Not that I cannot escape from police handcuffs. I will demonstrate, if you like. All the same, you little joke gave quite me a turn, and I suggest you take extra care where you sit. Shards of glass have a habit of hiding themselves right up to the moment they come into contact with flesh, and Hungarian crystal is especially vicious.

But to return to the case. As you surmise, I am indeed familiar with the trick of turning myself into my assistant and vice versa. Not only have I performed this astounding metamorphosis many times, I am, sir, its humble inventor.

Milk? Sugar? Garibaldi biscuit?

Permit me to familiarize myself once more with the facts. A gentleman by the name of Horace Brake, calling himself Marvo the Magician, set up in a church hall in Mill Hill. His first mistake, in my opinion. Church halls are dull, draughty places, totally ruinous to merriment and surprise, and dear me, to pick a Quaker Hall at that, what was he thinking? This is why the Great Rivorsky performs only in theatres, but Marvo is young, you say? Not yet twenty-five. The boy has much to learn.

Although I dare say he has figured out by now that it is virtually impossible to hypnotize a volunteer whose teeth are chattering from the cold.

And that the name Marvo the Magician smacks of a circus clown.

Cheap tickets, you say? Well, there you go. Another—what is it you English say?—clanger that young Marvo has dropped. A mere ten miles from London, it does not sound very far, but for the audience, it is out in the sticks. Folk will not travel that kind of distance for an amateur performance.

He might save on the costs, but equally he cannot hope to draw a sufficient crowd night after night to turn a profit, and in my business, Inspector, one simply cannot cut corners. Especially when travelling with an elephant. The idea is to make the beast disappear, not die of exhaustion, and of course once we reach our destination, we cannot rest on our laurels. A theatrical act requires meticulous preparation and continuous rehearsals, and there is always a backdrop to paint, a new costume to source, a new trick or routine to build in.

More tea?

Because by now you believe I am veering towards a verdict of accidental death. A consequence of youth, inexperience, greed and sloppy preparation, but I, Inspector, am not the Great Rivorsky for nothing.

My job is misdirection. Leading you believe one thing, before revealing the opposite.

The young lady in question was murdered.

• • • •

METAMORPHOSIS IS NO easy feat. The slightest slip, and the audience is bombarding you with distressed vegetable matter before you can say knife. Skidding on slimy cabbage when you're poised to turn into a woman is, take my word for it, no laughing matter.

Let me explain how the metamorphosis works.

The assistant, in this case a young lady named Thelma, ties Marvo to a wooden frame to which light, floaty curtains have been attached. He has already shown the audience, by lifting the curtains and moving his hand round, that there is nothing hidden inside or behind. Simply voile. Personally, I favour fabric similar to the petticoat you are sitting on at the moment, Inspector. Poor Greta, she must be shivering out there. But the point is, Thelma ties Marvo, arms outstretched, to the frame, and for good measure, fastens another bandage around his neck.

The frame is now folded in front of him, in the way that a bat folds its wings, a rope is passed round the entire contraption, then the whole caboodle is winched several feet in the air.

Thelma swirls Marvo's cloak, adds a few more theatricals, lifts the cape high so it hides her—and whoosh! When it swirls again, no more than two seconds later, it is not Thelma standing there, but Marvo. The contraption is now lowered back down, the rope is removed, the bat's wings are unfolded, and hey presto, as that snivelling corner-cutter Marvo would say, it is not the magician tied to the frame, but, *ta-da!*—his lovely assistant.

I see you are impressed. A hardened policeman, accustomed to the scams of con artists and the greasy fingers of pickpockets, you are nonetheless mystified as to how this could be achieved. And, dare I say, more than just a little in awe.

Of course, Marvo the Magician is perfectly capable of explaining the workings, but if you need me to enlighten you, it can only be because young Marvo is not around to do so himself. And you think that, because he has gone on the run, it is on account of his guilt.

That is was he who strangled Thelma and tied her to the frame.

Not so, sir.

I suspect, you see, that our impressario learned much of his dexterity from somewhat illegal activities. Bag-snatching, perhaps? An arrest for burglary? Either way, I'm sure you with this new-fangled fingerprint technology of yours, you will find him in your records, and not as Horace Brake, either.

Don't worry, Inspector. I'm sure he won't be on the loose for long.

In fact, I can tell you exactly where you will find this young man.

Along with the name of the person who murdered young Thelma.

. . . .

AH, INSPECTOR, COME in, come in, make yourself at home. Better weather today, don't you think? But then rain is invariably warmer than fog. Tell me, are there *ever* dry days in this country?

Yes, thank you for asking, Pepé's ankles are much improved after the poultice. Indeed, he is almost able to walk normally now. A slight pull to the left, but then again, he is Spanish. The audience expect nothing less.

From the glint in your eye, I deduce that you have run both young Marvo and Thelma's killer to ground. Excellent work, Inspector. Absolutely first rate. Me? No, no, no, no, no. I cannot take the credit for—oh, very well, a little. If you insist. Although it was plain as a pikestaff, once you understand how the trick works.

Like my disappearing elephant, the metamorphosis is nothing more than illusion. Young Marvo, and my apologies if the revelation came as a disappointment, never actually leaves the stage.

His assistant ties his hands with knots that appear impressively complex from a distance, but which, as any decent sailor would tell you, can slip free in an instant. Although I did have one dullard of a girl who could not rid herself of tying hitch knots, being raised on a farm and all that. I digress. The assistant secures his hands and neck to the frame and closes the bat wings. As they fold shut, he slips his hands free and unties the strap round his neck with his hands. While she ties the curtains together, he dismantles the front part of the frame, exposing a second assistant, already tied up, and dressed in identical clothes, wig and cosmetics as the girl on the stage. Long before Thelma secures the rope around the contraction, Marvo has taken himself and his frame through a door at the back that is obscured by cunning lighting and some rather ingenious mirror work.

What? Oh, the waving of wands and hands to prove there is only one flimsy curtain around the contraption? Basic quickness-of-the-hand deceiving the eye, I'm afraid. Like sawing the lady in half, there are very much two parts to this box. And, like the coffin I cut down the middle, the trick is to make it appear that it is only one piece.

With him out of the way, the box is duly winched in the air. Thelma does her swirly act with the cloak. A few extra theatricals. Then, ensuring the hem remains draped on the boards of the stage, she raises the cloak by its shoulder pads. Behind this sumptuous red velvet curtain, a trap door opens, Marvo jumps up, takes the cape, and at the same time Thelma disappears down the hole like greased lightning.

Timing, Inspector, is the key.

In the space of two seconds, Marvo has turned into his lovely assistant.

The dangling box is now lowered. The rope is released, the curtains untied, he unfolds the bat wings...and there, in the very place he himself had been secured, is his assistant.

As I say, he was on stage all the time. Two girls were made up to appear to be one. The only difference is that this time the poor child had been throttled.

Blue lips, a single half-open bloodshot eye, and the blackened tip of a tongue protruding through her teeth told him she was beyond medical help. At which point Horace Brake did what most young men who have had a brush with the law do. Legged it as fast as he could. Indeed, the only piece of luck he had going for him was that Quaker halls are notoriously underfilled. I believe your constable bandied an audience numbering seventeen? Quite. Not exactly the dogs of war on his heels.

On the other hand, where does a thief/burglar/pickpocket go with no money and only a morning suit stuffed with trick coins, decks of cards and collapsible props?

The answer lies in the Edgware, Highgate & London Railway line, but here his good fortune swung away. Even in thick fog, young men brandishing rabbits, paper swords and fake hands, and whose faces are slathered in theatrical make-up, are unlikely to slip quietly past the station guards. Those gentlemen have eyes that make hawks appear myopic, because hand on heart, Inspector, I was not trying to smuggle Mimi on board in the trick coffin without paying her fare. It was pure chance that she fell asleep without my noticing. And who could have anticipated Pepé would slink inside that empty trunk? Or eight of the company chose to pass themselves off as children? Genuine mistakes, sir, despite what the guard at Paddington claims. Which is why I say young Horace, kitted out in frock coat and greasepaint, had no chance of sneaking aboard without drawing attention, and yes. He might well be able to slip free of handcuffs. But not the armlock of a burly security guard, and I speak from experience on that one.

So you see, logic dictated that Marvo would be found in the local police cells. Desperate men don't go down without a fight, and Marvo-Horace-whatever his real name, was indeed desperate. A scoundrel through and through, in my opinion.

No, sir, not for stealing my illusion. After all, I *may* have seen something similar performed in Florence last year, which may, *possibly*, have found its way into my routine. And which would still form part of it, had my stage assistant not succumbed to the charms of Zorba the Freak, and found herself in the family way. They have asked me to be the baby's godfather, you know. What an honour, and when it arrives, the little imp will be a delightful addition to our happy troupe, but until then, it is impossible to pass off two females of differing girths as the same woman. That isn't metamorphosis, sir. That is farce.

Of course, the Great Rivorsky does farce exceedingly well—but that is for another time. You see, it occurred to me, while we were mulling over the case, that maybe Mill Hill wasn't such a careless and ill-advised choice. The unfortunate incident of my sawing the lady in half and leaving her feet, well Pepé's feet, still kicking made me think of my pilfering contortionist, which led me to pawnbrokers, which in turn led to me to wonder if that wasn't Marvo's game all along? There are, as I recall, several prosperous homes in the neighbourhood, and I suspect, when you check his previous venues, you will find that several houses have been broken into and robbed.

Where better for a jewel thief to hide than plain sight?

Ah. You have already found several glittery items among his personal effects? Splendid. Bang to rights, as you policemen say.

To celebrate, I think we should open this fine XO cognac. After forty years, the genie is impatient to get out of the bottle and who am I to deny him his freedom?

By this point, you probably fathomed out that it was not Thelma who died.

Thelma was on stage, busy tying up illusionists, waving their capes and sprinting down the stairs of the trapdoor like a rabbit whose powder puff tail is on fire. It was her double, the second assistant, who was strangled, and no, Inspector. For all his faults, Marvo would not have noticed when he stepped into the box. He would have been aware that she—Dolores you say her name was?—would have been strapped in beforehand, but given the tight timescale in which he must untie himself, dismantle the front section then dash out of sight, he would not so much as glanced at her face.

Watch, sir, as I re-enact the movements.

Left hand, right hand, quickly free the collar.

Click-click-click, there goes the collapsible frame.

One-two-three, as I roll up the false back drop.

I have barely time to turn, my arms stuffed full of wood and material, and slip behind the curtain and through the door, before the rope is tied and the box hoisted aloft.

And yes, I agree. Any one of the troupe could have murdered Dolores. But who, other than Thelma, had a motive?

• • • •

SHE WAS SHARING THE berth in Marvo's caravan, your notes said, and one suspects this was not for reasons of economic prudence. For very basic and professional reasons, magicians' assistants must be attractive. Their beauty, smile, slender form and mannerisms serve to distract the eye at critical moments. Well, yes. A flash of calf here, an exposed shoulder there doesn't hurt either, nor (and I am not ashamed to use the ploy myself) a saucy pose. Regardless of nationality, an audience expects a small degree of titillation. In short, they like to be shocked.

So although I have not seen the young lady in question, she would, by definition, be lovely. Just as Marvo who, until a run-in with the station guards ruined his good looks, would not have been without a certain *je ne sais quoi*. Sex-appeal is another weapon in the illusionist's armoury—why, thank you, Inspector, those are kind words—my point being that jealousy is a powerful motive.

More cognac? May I suggest you embrace the bowl of the glass in your hand to warm the amber nectar? Give it a swirl from time to time? You see how more pronounced the aroma, how deeper the flavour...

But as I was saying, in most instances, the green-eyed monster is neither myth nor illusion, though sadly in this case it was both.

Maybe Marvo loved Thelma, you will have to ask him yourself. Thelma most certainly fell hard for him. And when she sees him whispering furtively with Dolores, sneaking out to meet her in the dead of night, and catches the intensity of their conversation, if not the words, she fears she is being supplanted.

Knowing nothing about his lucrative sideline, how can she suspect that Dolores would be Marvo's partner in crime, instead of his lover? That such a sweet, innocent creature acts as lookout and scout, and is undoubtedly the one who sells their haul at the pawnbroker's shop.

All she sees is her man slipping out to meet with another woman at night.

And who comes home glowing with the unmistakable flame that only a rush of excitement can bring on.

Cigar, Inspector? They come all the way from Havana, thigh rolled I am told, and yes, indeed, it is a most elegant and unusual humidor. Black and lacquered, I have not seen anything to equal it. A gift long ago from my dear departed wife. No, no, not dead, sir. Just departed.

Poor Thelma, though. One cannot help but feel pity for her. Clearly not as much as the pity bestowed on Dolores. Dear me, no. But as the noose tightens round Thelma's neck—a certain irony, don't you think?—one cannot help but wonder why she felt the need to eliminate her rival by making it appear a stage accident.

Follow the girl down a dark alley, I say. Clobber her over the head with a good, solid piece of iron piping, and no one would look beyond robbery for the motive.

But then, the Great Rivorsky *is* an accomplished illusionist. Getting away with murder would be child's play for me.

A story I shall keep for another time...

A NIGHT IN CASABLANCA

"Of all the gin joints in all the towns in all the world, you booked me into this room?"

The desk clerk—Hans? Herman? something like that—could at least have *pretended* he'd never heard the line before. But he had one of those start-every-day-with-a-smile-and-get-it-over-with attitudes and programmed the key card with Germanic efficiency. Bea didn't care. Ten years on, she and Rusty were renewing their vows, so this wouldn't be just another raucous family get-together. Their idea was to host a wild mix of friends, work colleagues, all the hangers-on from before—in short, the wedding they *should* have had, if they hadn't been tied by tradition and nerves. She rubbed her hands. If this didn't turn into a night of drunken excess, bad behavior, and "pour decisions" (as Auntie Mamie would say), Bea would eat kale for a week.

"The Casablanca Suite is on the fifth floor, madam. Breakfast is in Tiffany's from 6:30 AM. Enjoy your stay."

Bloody right she would! They all would. Because where better to celebrate than the Hotel California, where each room was named for a place made famous by a classic movie? The Old Chicago Suite. The Midnight in Paris Suite. There was probably even an entire Philadelphia story....

"Yay! I'm in Suite Home Alabama."

"Can you promise me I *won't* be sleepless in Seattle?"

"If the lift breaks down, me and Jim will have to fly up to Rio."

The sour clerk was no match for these three shrieking millennials, the sisters of the bride, now reunited for the first time since Christmas. They wrapped Bea in a rugby-scrum hug, and their shrieking shot off the scale.

"Look!" one cried, just when the clerk thought things couldn't get any rowdier. "Auntie Mame!"

"Mamie!"

"Fabulous!"

"We weren't expecting you for another couple of hours."

The girls' aunt managed to embrace all four of her nieces in one scoop. "Are you kidding? Check-in's from two." She tilted her head toward the clock,

167

a replica of the one in *High Noon*. "Given the daily rate of this place, you didn't seriously think I'd miss a single second?"

Bea swore she heard the clerk's lip curl. "How was the train?" she asked, given Mamie's aversion to public transport.

"Lurching into the West End with one cheek pressed against a magazine dedicated to tire treads and alloy wheels while the other side of my face was offered insight into the intricacies of water treatment was educational, and I'm pretty sure a private jet would have been cheaper, but I'll live. Now, then. Who thinks we should start with Negronis?"

The vote was unanimous, as was the decision to sink them in the foyer, since they were merely the first wave of arrivals. Any second now, and—

"Annette! Karim!"

Right on cue, a wave of cousins, in-laws, co-workers, best friends, second-best friends—not to mention all those relatives no one really wanted to invite but no one was brave enough not to—rolled in through the swing doors, the side doors, and the lifts from the underground car park like a swarm of locusts. If noise pollution were a crime, the whole party would be locked up and the key thrown away, but so much had happened in the space of ten years: divorces, babies, break-ups, engagements, marriages, re-marriages, hirings, firings, disabilities, deaths. Catching up trumped check-in any day.

"—how Charles got promoted, I'll never know. That man would be out of his depth in a puddle—"

"—steer clear of Lois, mate. She's ruined more marriages than *Monday Night Football*—"

"—now *there's* a gene pool that could use a little more chlorine—"

A *frisson* of excitement rippled right down to Bea's hideously uncomfortable Jimmy Choos. Less than two Negronis in, the snitching and bitching was already in overdrive, and look! Uncle Dave was flirting with Kyle's second wife. Rusty's sister was doing what she did best: setting her sights on someone else's—anyone else's—husband. Ed from Accounts was using every inch of his charm to get into Ellie's knickers, without a clue that she was hot for Rebecca from Legal. And good old Rita, still hoping to shake down Uncle Matt.

Bea sighed happily. What a night this was going be!

"Helmut, we need champagne," Mamie yelled to the clerk. "Lots of it!" She turned to Bea. "Shame your mother couldn't be here, darling."

Bea glanced at the photographer, capturing every insult, snide remark, and suggestive comment on video. "I'm sure she'll be watching."

"Of course, darling, but it's not the same from prison. How long has she got left?"

Funny how corporate fraud never ends with a suspended sentence. "Five months yet till the parole hearing." Mamie was Bea's aunt on her father's side, which reminded her. "Don't suppose you've heard from Dad, have you?"

"Not a peep, sweetie, but with ten mill behind him I imagine it was easy for him to drop off the grid." Mamie sighed. "Typical of my baby brother to leave your mum carrying the can, but all his life he thought scruples were the little dangly bits at the back of his throat. And they were removed when he was six."

If Bea ever caught up with her father, there'd be more dangly bits at risk than just his tonsils. What kind of a man walks out on his family without so much as a word, leaving his wife to take the blame from, and his children to carry the shame of, his crime? But hey ho, all that was for another day—and she supposed there was always the possibility that her parents had *planned* it this way, one to slip cleanly away with the dosh while the other took the fall. The odds were that a woman would be sent to a minimum-security prison and have an easier ride—which, of course, was exactly what had happened. Who says romance is dead?

"Talking of absent friends"—Mamie squinted into the crowd—"where's that gorgeous husband of yours?"

Good question.

Bea frantically beckoned the clerk. "Horst, we need refills. These bottles are empty."

"Obviously, darling. It's dry champagne. Now stop changing the subject. Where's Rusty?"

"Upstairs, I think. Getting changed."

"Is that a euphemism for emptying the minibar?" Mamie gave her niece's cheek an affectionate pinch. "Oh, don't look so worried, sweetie. It's not called Dutch courage for nothing—and trust me, no self-respecting groom gets hitched without it, even the second time to the same woman. Or they could have given him the wrong room. Imagine, darling. You in Casablanca and poor Rusty in the Tara Suite—"

"Please don't say *in the bathroom, gone with the wind.*"

"My humor's too predictable, that's my trouble. You should still go and check on him, though." Mamie deftly caught the cork when it popped. "We can't have the male lead passing out before the ceremony, can we?"

No chance, Bea thought, pressing the button for the fifth floor. She and Rusty had agreed they'd have clear heads for their renewal vows. This was a serious matter, and in the crush downstairs no one had noticed that her lips barely touched her Negroni, or that she'd been wafting round with the same warm champagne in her flute for two hours. But keeping off the Tattinger to maintain a clear head was one thing. Not turning up for your own party was a bit much, even for workaholic Rusty.

"Wow!"

The Casablanca Suite was ten times better than Bea had imagined. Make that a hundred times. Spacious, luxurious, completely over the top—it was perfect. The walls were hung with publicity posters, head shots of Humphrey Bogart, Ingrid Bergman, Claude Rains, Peter Lorre, Sydney Greenstreet, Dooley Wilson, and Conrad Veidt, while piped-in music played...well, no prizes for guessing.

Bea tossed her case on the bed. No, not just perfect. The suite was absolutely *bloody* perfect, to be precise.

Rusty had picked the venue himself.

His words floated back to her: *We can't afford to fly everyone to Vegas and have some fake Elvis officiate, but that's no excuse not to make it cheesy. I read about this hotel....*

The Hotel California had been the brainchild, apparently, of Ronnie Kornblow of KornStar fame, a heavy-metal band from way back. Three of the five founding members succumbed years ago to sex, drugs, and rock 'n' roll, two of them dead by the age of thirty. Not Kornblow, though. Reinventing himself with the times, he was still recording, still full of ideas, still pushing boundaries, still making plans. Living proof that old rockers never die, they just "get" the blues.

You must remember this, a kiss is just a kiss....

Bea unzipped her suitcase and laid her dress on the bed.

Plan A had been to stick with white. Not the fluffy meringue she'd worn the first time, though, more a classy cocktail dress, all lace and straps, perhaps with little cap sleeves to keep it demure.

Then she thought, sod it, Rusty wanted this to be fun. *She* wanted this to be fun. Well, fun didn't come any funner than a traffic-stopping crossover red pencil number. Figure hugging, sultry, fiery, flirty—and slit far enough up the front to make Rusty's jaw drop to the floor. The same way he'd made hers drop, that night at Filipo's.

I've been thinking. His eyes sparkled as they chinked glasses, and there was a nervousness about him that no amount of candlelight could soften. Tense or not, though, he had never looked more handsome. *We'll have racked up ten years next month. Suppose we celebrate our anniversary by renewing our vows?*

And, OMG, he actually did the down-on-one-knee thing. *What do you say, Bea? Will you marry me again?*

"My ex's second cousin did that," Lisette had said, the next morning when Bea told her. Lisette was her assistant in the bakery, and, since they were assembling a three-tiered white-and-gold wedding cake at the time, it had seemed appropriate to bring up the subject of reruns. She fed Bea a string of roses to wrap around in a spiral. "Her husband took her hands in his and said, 'I pledged many things on our wedding day, including fidelity. I broke that vow, but I swear on everything I hold dear that you are the love of my life. With this locket, I reaffirm my commitment to you and this marriage.' Or words to that effect. I think he got the speech off the internet."

"Blimey, that was brave. Not many men would do that."

"It's apparently more common than you'd think." Lisette passed her the topper, a sparkly gold cutout that read *Together Forever*. "Trouble in this case was, up to that moment nobody knew that he'd been cheating on her." They stood back to admire their handiwork. "I tell you, Bea. No good ever comes from shagging other women, then owning up to salve your conscience. Their marriage didn't make it another week."

Lisette hadn't meant any harm. She was simply sharing. But the more Bea thought about it, the more she realized that Rusty *had* been working late a lot recently. Was away more often. And the new girl in the office just happened to be leggy, witty, and pretty....

It's still the same old story, a fight for love and glory....

He had pleaded the usual end-of-quarter reports, targets to meet, conferences, courses, meetings, conventions. But what else would he say? Bea hated herself for suspecting him. Cross her heart and hope to die, she felt bad, and once, when he left his phone on the kitchen table while taking out the rubbish, she'd been tempted to check. *Where's the harm,* she'd argued with herself, *if he has nothing to hide?*

Except that's not how trust works.

The fundamental things apply, as time goes by....

Perhaps she should have put her ethics aside, because once the seeds of doubt are sown, the roots quickly take hold. Rusty was organized and efficient, and it wouldn't be out of character for him to make amends for straying by renewing his vows in front of all and sundry.

"Sorry I cut it fine, Bea."

And there he was. As handsome as he had looked at Filipo's, that was nothing compared to now. All the tension that had been hanging over him these past two months—and had kept Bea from sleeping soundly—was gone. He was bouncing about like a kid on a trampoline, a boyish grin on his face. High octane didn't begin to describe it.

"Negotiations went right to the wire. I had to wrap the deal this morning, or we'd have lost it."

Bea slumped into a chair. He was lying. No one could walk into the Casablanca Suite without noticing the posters and photo on the walls, let alone the bright-red dress on the bed. She blinked back tears. There could be any number of reasons why Rusty was late, but deep down she knew: he was late because he'd finally had to end his affair. He'd probably tried, two, maybe even three months ago, before that night in Filipo's.

The cold air of certainty gripped her heart in a vise, and she swallowed the nausea rising inside her. Had whoever he'd been cheating with turned clingy? Had he felt rotten, leaving his unknown lover in tears every time, so he kept going back, hoping to make her feel better about the split? Maybe she'd felt led on and let down. Or had she turned bunny-boiling furious, threatening to confront his wife, post revenge porn on the web?

It didn't matter. The only thing that was relevant was that the weight had been lifted at last, and that's why Rusty was hyper.

I tell you, Bea. No good ever comes from shagging other women, then owning up to salve your conscience.

Her mother had put greed before family and had been locked up because of it. Her father was so crooked he could hide behind a spiral staircase—and his abandonment of his daughters was inexcusable. Whichever smart ass said that, sooner or later, everyone lets you down was spot on.

"Quick shower, then show time," Rusty said, grinning. "Isn't this suite great?"

Was it her fault? Had he turned to someone who was his intellectual equal, bored by a wife who worked in a bakery and opted for low pay and long hours over a nine-to-five office job? Bea made no secret of her passion for turning bags of flour into cupcakes, quiches, custard tarts, and cream buns. After all these years, she still got a thrill from watching dough magic itself into baguettes, flatbreads, and pizzas, from seeing eyes pop when customers "met" their wedding/birthday/christening cakes for the first time, so much more exciting than simply paging through photos in a book.

And that was the point. Nothing had changed for Bea, which was exactly why Rusty *would* be attracted to a girl with ambition. Someone whose go-getter lifestyle and go-getter pay matched his own, who understood PowerPoint and...and...all that other stuff.

Strangely, she could forgive him for tiring of her. She was stuck in a rut, while he was young and ambitious. But the one thing she could *never* forgive was the deceit. The sneaking around behind her back, pretending to be in places he wasn't—and then thinking that, because it was over, everything was suddenly all right again.

The *hell* it was—and suddenly her beautiful showstopper of a dress no longer symbolized passion. Now its red was the red of blood, blood bleeding from her broken heart....

On the wall across the room, Humphrey Bogart stared deep into Ingrid Bergman's eyes. The tag line on the poster read: "Casablanca...Where love cuts as deep as a dagger."

If Bea had a dagger, he'd see exactly how deep—

Then she heard Rusty whistling in the shower, not a care in the world, and in that moment she saw a path to a more satisfying—and less felonious—revenge.

Unlike their church service ten years ago, this time there'd be no separate processions down the aisle. This time, the happy couple would walk arm in arm between an archway of guests raising their glasses in a collective toast. There'd be a dais at the end, with a cake whose topper read *Better and Better*. It was all planned to the very last detail—but when it came to the moment for them to proclaim "I do...again!" to laughter and applause, Bea would pull an Eliza Doolittle and say, "Not bloody likely!"

She eased herself into the dress, smoothed on red Chanel lipstick, and thought, *Take that, you lying, cheap bastard.*

"That clerk on the front desk is a bad case of mistaken non-entity, and no mistake," Rusty called from the bathroom. "On my way up, I reminded him that the ceremony kicks off in the Moulin Rouge ballroom at seven sharp and asked if it was too late to change the guests' toasts for Manhattans instead of champagne. You'll never guess what the miserable git said."

If Rusty could put on an act, so could she. "No way, rosé?"

"I wish!" He stepped into the bedroom, toweling his hair. "If anyone needs a sense-of-humor implant, it's that bloke. He clicked around on his keyboard for a bit and said, 'Is there anything else you'd like changed at the last minute, sir?'"

All Bea had to do was hold her nerve for another twenty-one minutes.

"Anyway, you haven't heard the best bit. Coming upstairs, guess who I shared the lift with? Ronnie Kornblow. Seems he's between tours at the mo, and he offered to act as our witness!"

Better and better. With luck, the press would be there to record the event, and Rusty's humiliation would be complete. "What did your uncle say, when you told him he'd been supplanted by a rock star?"

Eighteen minutes.

"He was over the moon. Been dreading it, he said. Hey, you look amazing. If it wasn't for the fact that we've only got—"

"Seventeen minutes."

"—seventeen minutes, I'd ravish you on the spot."

That was the last straw, the last lie she'd ever let him tell her. Forget waiting for the ceremony, she'd have it out with the bastard right here, right now.

"I know what you've been up to."

Rusty's face fell. "Crap," he said. "I'm sorry, Bea. It was supposed to be—" He spiked his hands through his hair. "What gave it away?"

"This room, for one thing. You waltzed in here, didn't even gasp at how—"

"I know, I didn't think. It's just that I've been in here so many times—"

"You've *what*? You mean you brought your—"

"I scouted all hundred and seven rooms, but Casablanca was the one that kept drawing me back. I mean, it's perfect, right? Like your dress."

"My dress? You didn't even bloody *comment*, when you saw it on the bed!"

"Oh, God, I've really screwed up, haven't I? But I couldn't help myself, Bea. I took a peek in the spare wardrobe last night, and—full disclosure—that's why I switched the champagne toasts for Manhattans. So our cocktails would match your amazing outfit."

Seriously, if Rusty thought he could cover his ass with so-called scouting parties and red cocktails—

"Ten years ago, I promised to love you and honor you through sickness and in health, for better, for worse—and for the rest of our lives." He ran his hand over his anguished face. "But somewhere along the line, Bea, work overtook both of us. I've been promoted twice, which means more time away from you, while the bakery's gone from strength to strength, and you've had to put in longer and longer hours to make sure it stays that way."

"I love what I do."

"So do I, Bea. But I don't want our jobs to consume us, which is why—" He took a deep breath. "Don't be mad. I went behind your back, and maybe I shouldn't have been so sneaky, but how else could I spring the surprise?"

"What surprise?"

"It's been a nightmare, fitting six weeks of meetings into two, so I can take the time off. And then I had to find someone to fill in for you, which was another headache altogether."

He unzipped his suitcase and pulled out two passports and a sheaf of airline tickets. "First a night in Casablanca, and then a month in Marrakesh."

Someone squealed. Bea thought it must have been her.

"What do you say?" He dropped to one knee. "Will you honeymoon with me there again?"

She hugged him and kissed him, leaving red lipstick smears all over their faces. "Too bloody right, I will."

As it turned out, he'd packed for the trip for both of them. The cases were at Reception, and their flight was scheduled for tomorrow afternoon. How he managed to dress and get them downstairs with only three minutes to spare was beyond her, but as they walked through the archway of red Manhattans towards a minister and a rocker in leathers, both grinning from ear to ear, Bea thought her heart would burst.

The desk clerk had changed the guests' toasts for cocktails, as instructed, but not the champagne on the dais. Ronnie Kornblow poured them each a flute and one for himself. Champagne flutes and cocktail glasses chinked in orchestral harmony, everyone drank to their health—and almost instantly the guests began to throw up.

Horrified, Bea and Rusty watched their guests spew for England.

"This is Heinz's doing!" Bea said, sure that, this time, her instincts were right. "Somebody call 9-9-9!"

The three of them raced to Reception. The desk clerk saw them and made a break for the exit, but Ronnie brought him down with a flying tackle as the paramedics and police flooded in.

"I'm not sorry," the clerk shouted, his voice muffled by the middle-aged rocker's bulk crushing him to the carpet. "I'm put upon again and again by the guests in this bloody hotel. No one acknowledges me, they don't tip, they don't smile. They don't even get my bloody name right. Well, now the whole world will know my name!'

Or perhaps not. Even Ronnie, the man's boss, couldn't remember it. He had hundreds of employees and was rarely on site. The other staff didn't like the creepy sod and avoided him like the plague. Horst? Hugo? Something German, anyway. Even the news media got it wrong, confused the bloke with some guy who'd murdered three hotel managers a few months back.

Anyway, the incident barely rated a paragraph in the *Evening Herald*. A resentful nobody slipped an emetic to a rowdy crowd that was already drunk, and no one was actually harmed? Who really cared?

Late that night in the Casablanca Suite, Bea and Rusty pledged their eternal love through a haze of champagne. But all they really remembered in the years to come was that sea of red vomit...and the marvelous Moroccan month that followed.

Ingram Content Group UK Ltd.
Milton Keynes UK
UKHW011830170323
418736UK00004B/247